AWAY GAME

CATHRYN FOX

NEW YORK TIMES BESTSELLING AUTHOR

COPYRIGHT

Discover other titles by Cathryn Fox at www.cathrynfox.com. Please sign up for Cathryn's Newsletter for freebies, ebooks, news and contests: https://app.mailerlite.com/webforms/landing/c1f8n1
ISBN ebook : 978-1-989374-50-4
ISBN Print 978-1-989374-49-8

1

CHASE

I know we get bad storms in Boston, but come on, this is ridiculous. I lean forward and peer out my icy window, but I can barely see two feet in front of my Jeep. My wipers are on high, yet they're unable to keep up with the heavy flakes coating my window. Everything from my vehicle to the road and trees are covered in inches of thick, wet snow, making this journey treacherous, and nearly impossible.

I drive by a sign on this narrow back road in Nova Scotia, but it's whited out and unreadable. Even if the words were visible, I'm not from around these parts, so it wouldn't mean much to me. Still, I'd like to at least know my whereabouts, should I go flying off some cliff and somehow—miraculously—survive.

Seriously though, I have no idea where I am, or if this winding road leads to Halifax. Christ, I've never heard of the Trans-Canada highway shutting down before, the four-lane freeway completely impassable, forcing drivers to take these backwoods detours. Then again, I've never been in stormy Nova Scotia during the dead of winter either.

If I had it my way, I'd be back in Boston at the dorm, getting ready to fly home for three days, for a short break before we gear up for the playoffs, but I had no choice in the matter. This is the only time I could join the Scotia Storms for practice and decide whether I want to stay and play hockey at Boston University or join the Storms, a top Atlantic university hockey team in Halifax.

My buddy Brandon raves about the Scotia Storms—now I see where they get their name—and the top-notch education at the Academy. He says the downtown nightlife has a great vibe, with genuine people, and the city, by far, has the hottest women on the planet. I don't really believe that. I think it's just his way to lure me here. Although Brandon would never lie to me. The two of us go way back to our kindergarten years. Our dads played together for the Seattle Shooters, and yes, we both feel the pressure that comes with our father's high levels of achievement.

But speaking of Brandon, he could have at least warned me that the roads were going to be deadly. Last I heard there were over fifteen-hundred vehicles stranded on the Trans-Canada. Shit, he probably thinks I'm one of them and is no doubt worried sick. No way can I take my hands off the wheel or eyes off the road to message him and I don't dare pull over in these conditions. It's a total white out. I can't even tell where the road ends and the ditch begins. Not that I think I'd have service out here in the middle of nowhere—and yes, it's true, I'm the only idiot on this particular back road.

I grip the steering wheel tighter and blink, trying not to get snow hypnosis and veer into a tree. I turn my high beams on and off. It does nothing to help with my visibility. The road curves and I ease off the gas to coast around the turn. From my peripheral vision, I spot movement and shoot a fast glance to my right. What the hell was that? I adjust my rearview mirror and catch a flash of something...or someone. I pinch my eyes shut and open them again. I must be imagining things. No one would be standing on the side of the road in the middle of a storm...unless.

I slow to a stop, and back up. My tires spin the whole way, and when I see movement again, I shove my Jeep into park and hop out. My boots sink into the snow, slowing me down. I circle my vehicle and that's when I realize there's a car in the ditch, and my spraying tires just soaked someone standing a few feet away from the vehicle's flashing brake lights. I quickly take in his splayed arms, and the way he's gasping as slush drips from his winter coat.

"Are you okay?" I yell, but my words get carried away in the wind. I step closer to the motionless figure, and come face to face with Frosty the Snowman. Technically it's a person, but all that's missing to complete the children's beloved character is the carrot nose. You know what's not missing? The eyes made out of coal. Yeah, that's right. This guy has two black eyes peering out from a snowy hood tugged tight and if looks could kill I'd be a goner. I'm guessing he's not about to come to life and spread good cheer. Can't say I blame him. "I'm sorry. I didn't mean to soak you."

"It's okay. It's not your fault, but dammit, isn't this day just getting better and better," the guy—or rather the girl—says as fat snowflakes coat her lashes.

My gaze races over her shivering body, as she shifts from one foot to the other. She's all bundled up so I can't tell if she's injured from the crash. "Are you hurt?"

She wraps her arms around herself and her breath turns to fog as she speaks. "No, just cold and wet and late."

I understand late. I pull my phone from my pocket to check for service. Zilch. Not only that, I'm down to one bar. "Do you have service?"

"No. I can't even call for a tow truck, and the closest town is a few miles down the road. I don't think I can make it on foot."

At least one of us knows where we are. I'm grateful for that. I shake my head as a cold shiver goes through me. "Here I thought I was the only idiot on this side road."

"Did you just call me an idiot?"

"What, no." Way to make a first good impression, Chase. "I didn't mean that. I'm the idiot. I should have turned back instead of taking the detour." I gesture with a nod to my Jeep. "You'd better get in and we need to get off the road before someone takes that corner too fast and crashes into us."

"I..." She glances at the tail end of her car sticking out of the ditch, the brake lights fading to black. She groans and looks back at me. It's easy to tell she's not comfortable climbing into a car with a stranger. I don't blame her.

"I'm not a serial killer," I say, hoping to ease her worries.

"Which is exactly what a serial killer would say, but under the circumstances, I'm safer with you than in this storm." She eyes me for a second, like she's committing my features to memory. "Just so you know, I know judo."

I hold my hands up, palms out. "Duly noted."

I shuffle my feet in the snow to make a path for her, and she follows me to the passenger side. I open the door, and a burst of snow follows her in. My gaze moves over her for a second. How the hell did I think she was a guy? She's so petite, it's a surprise her feet reach the floor. Once she's secure, I trudge through the wet snow again and climb into the driver's side, cranking up the heat to melt the snow covering her coat.

She tugs off her mitts and holds her quivering hands over the vents to warm them, and I resist the urge to take them in mine and create heat with friction. That would be inappropriate, and something tells me she'd judo me right in the nuts.

"I am so cold." I flick on the heated seat and after a few moments, she wiggles. "Oh, that is so nice."

As soon as we're both buckled up, I cast her a quick glance. "Ready?"

She nods, and I glance around to make sure the road is clear behind me before I hit the gas. My wipers squeal as they struggle with the snow and I lean forward to concentrate on the road. "How far did you say the next town was?"

"Just a couple miles. Not much there, but there is a gas station, and a small motel. It could be full, or shut down. Storms like these tend to knock out the power for days."

Shit. "I don't have days." I had plans to join the guys on the ice and check out the academy's curriculum to figure out if I want to pack up my life in Boston and move to Canada. By the looks of things right now, I'm going to miss a few days that I can't afford to miss. The coach isn't going to want a guy on the team who can't show up on time. I just hope Brandon talks to him and can postpone our meeting.

"Me neither." She groans and looks out the window.

"What are you late for?"

"I was meeting a friend Lily in New Brunswick and tomorrow we're supposed to fly to Florida for the holidays. Her parents have a place there." A shiver goes through her as the cold leaves her body. "I was so looking forward to the warm weather."

"Warm weather would be nice right about now."

She takes a deep breath and lets it out slowly as she looks in the side view mirror. "I suppose it could be worse. I could have died in the crash."

"Hey, way to look on the bright side." She turns and practically snarls at me. I bite back a grin. "Too soon?"

"Too soon," she says and grumbles something about her father warning her about the weather and how she was sure she could beat the snow and that I was right—she's is an idiot.

"They weren't calling for this much snow, which is why I decided to drive to New Brunswick and fly out with Lily," she explains like she's trying to justify her actions.

"Meteorologists," I tease. "The only thing they get right is it's light today and dark tonight."

She chuckles at that, and the sweet sound wraps around me.

"True, but the weather can be unpredictable here in Nova Scotia this time of year."

I think it's sweet that she's standing up for the meteorologists, especially after veering off the road. My heart softens as I take in her disappointment. "I'm sorry you're missing your trip. Can you reschedule for Monday? Catch another flight?"

She laughs, almost manically. Maybe I should be the one worried about her being the serial killer.

"You're obviously not from around here."

"Boston," I state, and when she arches a brow, I continue with, "I'm meeting a buddy in Halifax for the February break." I don't bother telling her who I am and the real reason I'm heading to the city. People instantly change when they find out my father was in the NHL, and that I'm his little prodigy who is expected to live up to the hype. I hate it, all of it. The expectation. The girls who want me because I play hockey. I can never tell who's real and who isn't, who likes me because I can sink a puck, and who likes me just for me. It's honestly kind of nice chatting with someone who has no idea who I really am.

All that will change when I reach the city—I'll be introduced around as Chase Adams, a lightning fast forward with great leadership skills, drafted at eighteen and expected to head to the NHL after college. But for right now, I'd like to be incognito and maybe we can just be two strangers who don't have to know anything about each other and can become friends. Although that's a bit ridiculous. I probably won't set eyes on her again.

She nods. "If you were from around here, you'd know that it's going to take days to get plowed out, especially up here on the mountain."

I nod. I thought I was climbing on this back road, but it was hard to tell. "My name is Chase," I tell her, not bothering to tell her my recognizable last name. Then again, Adams is a common name and she might not put two and two together and realize Jamie Adams, former player for the Seattle Shooters, is my father.

"Nice to meet you, Chase. I'm Sawyer." I note that she doesn't bother giving me her last name either. I've never met a girl named Sawyer before, and I dig the name. "I'd shake your hand, but I don't want you to take yours off the wheel."

"Good call." She goes quiet for a second and I can almost feel the disappointment rolling off her.

"I'm glad you're not hurt, and your car didn't look too banged up. It's probably still drivable, once we get it towed out."

She turns and I catch her smile in the dashboard lights. "Thanks for stopping. I don't know what I would have done." She laughs and adds, "You're my knight in shining armor, or rather, my knight in a down filled jacket and a four-wheel steed with heated seats."

I smile but it scares me to think how easily I could have overlooked her. Thank God I turned my head when I did. "I barely saw you."

She snorts, like I touched on a sore spot. "Yeah, the story of my life."

"What?"

"Nothing. Ignore me. My brain is frozen." She spends a good five minutes trying to undo the knot on the string of her hood. After a few mumbled curses, she gets it undone and pulls it off. I steal another quick glance at her. Holy shit. If someone had told me I was going to rescue the most beautiful woman on the planet, I would have told them they were nuts. Maybe Brandon wasn't lying about the beautiful women, after all. In the dashboard light, I take in her long wavy hair, dark as the night surrounding us.

I force my eyes back on the road—even though I want to keep looking at her longer. How could I have thought she was a guy. From my peripheral vision, I catch the way she fans out her long hair before she ties it into a ponytail. She unzips her coat, and I take in a big sweater that hugs her breasts. She groans as she tugs at her pants.

"Soaked?" I ask.

"Yeah, and all my clothes are in my suitcase, and we know where my suitcase is." Her shoulders sag. "Although I don't think I have any use for a bikini anymore. But we could be stranded for days, and I don't have a change of clothes."

Oh shit, now I'm envisioning her in a bikini.

Concentrate on the road, Chase.

She goes quiet for a moment and stares out the window, deep in thought. What is going through her mind? After a moment, a laugh bubbles out of her, and under her breath she murmurs, "At least I'm in clean underwear."

What the hell?

My throat makes a gurgling sound as I force my thoughts on the road, and not what she's wearing beneath those tight jeans.

Her eyes go wide, and that's when I see her innocence. I let my gaze roam over her face for another split second. There's something very different about her. I think she's giving off a girl-next-door wholesome vibe. At least, this is what I think innocence looks like. I don't see much of it in the puck bunnies who watch us from the bleachers and chase us down after a game.

"Oh, sorry. I don't know why I said that. I guess, it's just... something my mom used to say." She laughs but it's forced. "Always wear clean underwear in case you're in an accident." She shakes her head, like she's flustered. "I mean, I always wear clean underwear. I wasn't suggesting I didn't."

"Oh, sure yeah. I didn't think that at all. I wear clean underwear too."

Why the hell did I say that? Oh, maybe to make this exchange just a little less awkward.

"Oh, God," she mumbles, and shakes her head. While I think she looks adorable, it appears like she wants to jump out of my moving vehicle and run all the way to the motel—or Siberia. She points to her head. "And clearly I'm still suffering from a frozen brain and have no idea what I'm saying."

My gaze sways her way and I glance down at her tight jeans. Jesus, I wish she'd stop rambling on about her underwear, because now I can't stop thinking about what they might look like on her body, or better yet...off.

Isn't this day just getting better and better?

Why yes, yes, it is...

2

SAWYER

What the hell is wrong with me? Why on earth would I talk about my underwear in front of a stranger?—a hot one at that. Here I was worried he might be a serial killer and now, no doubt, he's worried he picked up an escaped mental patient who has a fascination with her own underwear.

He inches the zipper down on his coat, like he's a bit uneasy with the direction of my conversation—it's the only logical explanation, considering the car is cold and he can't be hot— and I bite back a pained, embarrassed laugh and lean my head back against the headrest to get myself together. It's true, I have a tendency to ramble when I'm uncomfortable. I was fine right up until he turned my way and I caught his features in the dashboard light.

Holy hotness.

Trust me, I've been around numerous hot guys, on campus and at the rink, but the sight of his hard, unshaven jaw and arctic blue eyes warmed my frozen body faster than the heated seat hugging my backside did. Lessons learned, however, have taught me that guys like him don't go for girls like me—for numerous reasons. So, it's best not to fantasize about a snowed in weekend with Mr. America. Okay, well, I mean I can fantasize. I'm just not going to. Much.

Groaning under my breath, I pull my phone from my pocket and pretend I'm reading messages from a hot boyfriend, who doesn't exist. The reality is, the only messages are old ones from my best friend Lily, who is waiting for me in New Brunswick, my dad, members of my curling club, and a few from students in the theater department at Scotia Academy. God, could I be any more boring? Chase here probably dates cheerleaders, like the ones who parade themselves in front of the team my dad coaches.

"Service?"

His voice pulls me back, and I shake my head. "Nothing." I wipe my hand over the passenger side window to clear the condensation, but it's getting darker and darker, and I can't see a thing.

"We must be getting close," I say, judging by how long we've been driving.

"Up there. I see something." I take in the relief in his voice, as I lean forward and spot the big Folly Mountain Motel sign on the edge of the road, the vehicle's headlights bouncing off it.

The motel comes into view, and it's mostly dark. "I don't think they have power."

"At least it's somewhere to stop and get out of the storm."

"Hey, way to look on the bright side of things." He grins and I continue with, "Are you a glass half full kind of guy?" Truthfully, I am too, but I'm just so disappointed. I've been saving forever for this trip. I had big plans that are quickly circling the drain.

"Right now, I'll take a half a glass of anything."

I nod in agreement. "Yeah, I'm thirsty too, and hungry." I have water and snacks back in my car, but I was too worried about my vehicle exploding after I crashed, so I hightailed it out of the driver's seat with only my purse.

He slowly eases off the road and plows through the heavy snow in front of the motel. As he passes a few parked vehicles, his Jeep begins to slide and I gasp. Instinctively, I reach out and grasp his arm to hold on to. He pumps the brakes until he gets the Jeep under control and I let out a sigh.

"Are you okay?" he asks.

"I think I'm more shaken up than I realized."

His brow furrows. "I can't even imagine, Sawyer."

"I was driving carefully, and started spinning out on that curve." I briefly close my eyes as the scene plays out before my eyes. "The next thing I knew my air bag went off, and I was face down in a ditch." I touch my face, right around my eye. "Oww."

"You're hurt."

"I didn't even know it until now."

"Adrenaline," he explains.

I nod. He must be right, because all of a sudden, I'm so tired I'm not even sure I have the strength to walk inside the dark motel. Chase eases his car into a parking space—not that we can tell if it's a designated spot—and kills the ignition. I glance around at the other snow-covered vehicles.

"I hope they're not full," he says, as he zips his coat back up.

"They probably won't turn us away, even if they are."

"Really."

I laugh. "You're in Nova Scotia, Chase. We're all nice, and hospitable and say sorry a lot."

He laughs at that, and it helps to ease some of the tension inside me. "My buddy said you were all genuine." He reaches for his door handle. "Come on, let's go check it out." He pushes his door open, shoving snow with it, and steps out. I try my door, but I don't have his strength. He grabs a bag from the backseat, circles the car and comes to my side. With a good hard yank, he has my door open and reaches for my hand.

"I've never seen snow this deep before."

"Folly Mountain," I explain. "Worst place to be in a storm, and I think this one is for the record books."

"I'd say the Trans-Canada is the worst place to be in a storm."

I laugh and go on to explain. "We call it the Cobequid pass and the worst place to build a highway. Seriously bad weather conditions in a storm. Trucks jackknife in nearly every big storm and cars pile up. We're both lucky we got off it when we did."

"I took the exit at the last second."

"Same. Not idiots after all, eh?" I say with a laugh.

Snow falls over us, and our coats are white in record time as we try to plow our way through the parking lot to the front door. I peer inside and see nothing but flickers of lights as Chase pulls the door open and gestures for me to enter first.

I watch a lot of scary movies, so this kind of creeps me out, but he's being a gentleman, not making me go in first because I'm bait for some monster.

"Hello," I call out as I enter, and a head pops up from a sofa near the fireplace. "Hello," I call out again, and the figure slowly rises from the sofa, and comes toward us.

"Oh my, look at you two," an elderly woman exclaims as she gets close. She holds up a battery-operated pillar candle encased inside some kind of wire cage. She examines us, and in turn I take in her features and the lines around her eyes as they narrow with concern. She looks to be in her late seventies, and I can't tell if she's wearing a robe, or what my grandmother used to call a house dress. She waves her gnarled hands. "Get in here."

We both kick the snow off our boots and brush off our jackets before we step inside. "Do you have any rooms?"

"You're in luck. We have two left."

If I wasn't so hungry and stressed, I'd laugh at that. In every romantic comedy I've ever watched, when a guy and girl get stranded, there's only ever one room left at the inn. But this isn't a romantic comedy and while Chase might be my hero for picking me up on the side of the road, I'm no one's heroine.

"Thank God," Chase says. He pulls his phone out. "Do you have service?"

"Sorry, I have a battery powered radio." She fusses with some dials, and songs from the last century fill the lobby. "All I can offer you is a bed, and something to eat."

"Food," I moan—extremely unladylike I know, but we're in trying times here. From behind me, Chase chuckles, the warmth of his breath on my ear.

"The cafe is open?" he asks, somewhat surprised.

"No, but there's already made sandwiches and bagels and pie. None of it will last long with the power out, so help yourselves." She looks us over. "Do you have any luggage?"

"I do," Chase answers and shrugs the shoulder he has his bag on. "Sawyer's car is in the ditch a couple miles down the road."

"Oh, no." She takes my cold hand into her warm one. "Are you okay, dear?"

"I am."

She holds the light over me. "Perhaps I can find a few things for you to wear. They might be a bit big on you, but they'll do in a pinch."

"That's so sweet, thank you."

"Now come with me. Let's get you both checked in and you can go to the café." She points to a hallway off the main lounge area. "It's just down that hall." She circles the counter, pulls out a book to write our names in, and I guess she's going old school since her computer is down, until I see the names and past dates of other guests as well. I grin to myself.

"Do you own this place?" I ask and she beams.

"It's been in the family for generations. My Billy and I took it over when Dad passed some twenty years ago." I glance around, searching for Billy, but maybe he's gone to bed already, or maybe he's...gone. Either way, I don't bring him up.

"Do you have a landline?"

"Yes, each room has a phone. Everyone has a cell now, but we keep the landlines for emergencies like these. I called Malcolm and he said the power is out all over the mountain us, and we might not see a plow for days."

"Malcolm?"

She beams. "Our son. He's an RCMP officer."

"Do you think we could use the phones in our rooms to let our friends and family know we're safe and off the road? It's long distance."

"Be my guest. The cost will just be added to your bill, dear," she says. "I also have spare flashlights for guests. It's not uncommon for us to lose power in these kinds of storms. I have a generator, but Billy hasn't been able to get it working for ages."

She hands each of us a flashlight and relief goes through me. I can at least let Dad and Lily know I'm safe and off the roads. I should probably tell Lily to go on to Florida without me. I'm not getting out of this place for days. Sorry, hymen, I guess you'll have to stay intact for a little bit longer.

"Thank you...uh...Mrs...."

"Betsy. It's just Betsy."

I smile at Betsy, who reminds me of my own dear grandmother on my dad's side. We lost her a while ago, and my grandmother on my mother's side, too. Well, when Mom ran off with Dad's best friend, my maternal grandmother had little to do with Dad or me. I wonder if Mom wore clean underwear when she hopped into the car with Dad's assistant coach and drove to Alberta, never to be heard from again.

That ridiculous thought hits like a fist to the gut. It's been years since I've seen or heard from my mother, yet the fact that she left without so much as a wave good-bye still hurts.

The sound of a heavy drawer scraping open as Betsy pulls out two keys has me shelving thoughts of my mother. She doesn't deserve to pass through my brain, nor does she deserve my tears. Betsy dangles two keys hanging from plastic keyholders. Like actual metal keys. Not the swipe card kind from the twenty-first century, and I suppose that's good. They wouldn't work without power. But you know what, I'm not really thinking about that right now.

How can I when Chase is standing so close to me, the heat of his body wrapping around me and doing the weirdest things to my insides? As he accepts his key, I angle my head and try to get a better look at him without getting caught. He's tall, that much I already knew. He towered over me when he stood next to me on the side of the road, but he's big and solid too, and I'm sure it's not just his winter coat over exaggerating his build. My gaze goes to his big hands, and for some ridiculous reason, I imagine them on my body, touching, exploring parts of me that no man has ever touched before. Maybe he could be the no strings hook-up I intended to have in Florida. Hey, it's not that I want to remain a virgin forever, it's just that—

"Sawyer?"

I blink. "What?" Shit, I was so lost in my fantasy I missed what he said to me.

He gestures with a nod toward Betsy. "Your key."

"Oh, right sorry." I take the key and squeeze it in my palm.

Get yourself together, girl.

"Brain still frozen?" he asks, as blue eyes assess me with concern. My God, he's so genuine and serious, and so adorable for thinking it's the cold that's throwing me off, I can't help but grin at his naivety. Or maybe he's just used to women ogling him and he's cutting me some slack instead of calling me out about it. Either way, I'm grateful.

"Something like that."

Betsy points to the stairs. "Those stairs will lead you to your rooms, and you can use the landlines to call your family."

"Thank God for old technology," I murmur to Chase as I flick on my flashlight and head toward the stairs. Chase follows closely, leaving his flashlight off. Good call. We don't want to run out of batteries. I turn to admire the fire lighting up the foyer. Maybe once Betsy finds me some dry clothes, I can change and relax in front of it. It's not like there's much else I can do to pass the time. "Do you think they have marshmallows?"

Chase shrugs one broad shoulder. "We can ask."

We.

Oh, so he's going to join me. I like that far too much.

"I take it you like camping," he says as we go up the stairs and I try not to sound breathless—which has nothing to do with the steep steps. Chase doesn't seem bothered or winded by the long climb. Why would he? He's in great shape. We reach the landing, and he walks beside me.

"Hate it."

He arches a brow. "You've done it?"

"Of course, I've done it. Sleeping on the ground is not for me, and for the record, I'm not one of those people who say they hate something when they haven't done it. That's so annoying."

He laughs. "I totally agree. My buddy on the te—" He stops abruptly. "Just this friend of mine. He says he hates lobster, but has never tasted it."

"He's missing out."

"I can't wait to try some Nova Scotia lobster."

"Well, you've not tasted anything until you had one of my roasted marshmallows."

He grins. "You really like marshmallows, huh?"

"Come on, who doesn't?" I rub my stomach. "S'mores. It's like a whole food group."

"True." He grins. "I like camping. My folks have a place in Washington. Wautauga Beach. I spent a lot of time there as a kid. Lots of bonfires and s'mores."

"But this place...the beach...you slept in a tent?"

He laughs. "Okay, you got me there. It was a beach house."

I nudge him, and he doesn't move. "That's roughing it, Chase."

"We even had a stocked lake nearby, but the only thing I ever caught was a fly bite or two."

I laugh at that as a cute grin showcases one big dimple on his left of his cheek. I bet he gets freckles around his nose in the summer too.

"Wait, a beach house in Washington is kind of far from Boston, isn't it?"

"Yeah, uh, well my parents are still in Seattle. I went to Boston for college."

"Oh, I see." My gaze rakes over his face. I don't know him very well, but I sense there's a story there, one he's not about to share with a stranger, and that's okay. His business is none of mine, but that doesn't stifle my curiosity one little bit. We stop outside room 212, and I point. "This is me."

"That's me," he says and points to the room right beside me. Maybe we'll have adjoining doors. I roll my eyes at that thought. Why would that matter? I probably won't spend another second alone with him from here on out.

He pauses for a second. "Come get me after you make your calls, and we'll go grab something to eat."

Or maybe I will.

3

CHASE

I turn on my flashlight and fumble with my key, working to fit it into the lock as Sawyer does the same beside me. I angle my head to see her, and while it sucks that she's going to miss her trip, I can't deny that I like her company. It's odd really. I'm a bit of a loner, an introvert, a guy who likes to keep to himself, and I'm sure I've talked more in the last fifteen minutes than I have in the last week. Why the hell did I tell her about my parents' beach house? I don't normally talk about personal things like that, and if I'm trying to go incognito this weekend, it's best I don't reveal anything more about my life.

Of course, she'd be the only one who knows nothing about me. While it pains me to be in the public eye, my life on display for all to scrutinize, on the ice I keep my head down and tune out the audience. It's the interviews that kill me and leave me feeling drained and exhausted. I usually need a couple of hours to myself to refill my energy after being in the spotlight. The only one who knows that about me is my buddy, Brandon.

"Need a hand?" I ask Sawyer, trying not to chuckle as she mumbles curses and kicks her door. Like that's going to help, but she's frustrated with this turn of events. I'd probably kick my door too, but I can't say I'm as upset as she is.

She casts me a glance, just as her key turns in the lock. "Got it," she says, and disappears into her room. After a bit of a struggle as well, I finally get my key into the old lock that could use a little lubricant. I shove the door open and once inside I sweep my flashlight around to take in the small room with the queen bed. The furnishings are old, the TV ancient, but the space is still warm and has a place to lay my head and a working bathroom, and that's all I need tonight. Okay, that might be all I *need*, but it's not all I *want*. I briefly close my eyes and envision sweet Sawyer on my bed, and my dick thickens in my unforgiving jeans.

What the hell is wrong with you, dude?

I get that I'm a guy and she's a beautiful girl I just met, but I've been so busy, focused on hockey and school, I can't remember the last time I had a warm body next to me. Sex is nice, but unlike the other guys on my team back in Boston, it's not a daily necessity. Although maybe I *should* make it a priority. Maybe that would help alleviate the pressure on me to succeed in hockey and school. Back in Boston I'm studying business, like most of the other guys on the team. It's a good degree, employable, but deep down it's not what I want to do with my life after the NHL—if I even make it to the big leagues. Heck, being drafted doesn't guarantee I'll make it, and being the son of a former super star just puts more pressure on me to succeed.

I drop my bag, stretch out my tired arms and plunk myself down on the edge of the bed. I grab the phone on my night-stand and punch in Brandon's number. Thank God I actually know it. He answers on the first ring, and sounds completely anxious when he says, "Chase, bro, where are you? Are you okay?"

At least it's nice to know he was worried about me. I guess I can forgive him for not telling me about the treacherous Trans-Canada, or as Sawyer called it, the Cobequid pass, and like she said, the weather this time of year is unpredictable. I shake my head. I've known her for less than an hour, yet I find myself wanting to think about her, wanting her name on my lips. Wanting my tongue on her body.

Whoa, cool it, Chase.

"I'm good. I'm at some motel on Folly Mountain."

He blows out a breath. "Are you okay? You sound strange."

I clear my throat. "Just tired. It's been a long day."

"It's a good thing you got off the highway or it would have been an even longer night. Those drivers are going to be stranded until morning, maybe even longer."

I walk to the window and pull back the curtain to take in the heavy flakes still falling. "I'm on some back road and I'm guessing those on the highway will get plowed out before me."

"Shit, really?"

"There's more snow up here than on the Trans-Canada. I could be snowed in for days."

"Fuck. You don't have days to waste."

"I know," I say but there's this tiny part of me that doesn't hate the idea of taking a break from life for a quick minute. I've been groomed for hockey since I was old enough to put on a pair of skates. Don't get me wrong. I love the sport. Playing is when I'm happiest, but sometimes the pressure is pretty severe. My buddy Brandon knows exactly what I'm talking about. He's the only guy I've ever confided in and vice versa.

"Do you think Coach Jameson is going to be pissed?"

"I think Coach Jameson is going to worship the ground you walk on, Chase," he replies with a laugh. "Don't worry about him. I'll explain everything. Have you talked to your folks?"

"No, they're my next call. Then I'm going to grab a bite to eat." I don't bother telling him about Sawyer. I don't know why exactly We share everything, but there's something inside me that wants to keep her to myself for now. My life is an open book—not by choice—but as the hockey playing son of an NHL superstar, my life is documented for all to see. I like that Sawyer doesn't know who I am. I'm guessing she doesn't follow hockey.

I yawn, and Brandon says, "Get some rest, and keep me posted. I'll get a hold of Coach for you."

"Thanks, buddy."

I hang up, and the next call is to my parents. As I fill them in, and promise to keep them updated, I end the call and flop down onto my bed, rolling to the middle. I'm guessing this place hasn't changed their mattresses since the early forties. But I'm not about to complain.

A knock comes on my door, and I push myself from the bed, hoping it's Sawyer, ready to get something to eat. I'm starving, but that's not the only reason I hurry across the floor like a schoolboy with a crush.

I peer through the peephole, and realize the knock wasn't at my door. It's Betsy bringing Sawyer clothes. Since the walls are paper thin, it's easy to listen to the exchange. The hall goes quiet again and I change into a pair of dry pants, giving Sawyer time to get out of her wet clothes and come to my door. I wait for a good twenty minutes and when she doesn't show, I snatch my key from the dresser and head to her room. I knock, and hear movement, but she doesn't come to the door. A strange sense of panic invades my gut. I knock harder.

"Sawyer. Is everything okay?"

"No," she says her voice right there, on the other side of the door, like she was standing there the whole time. Maybe she doesn't want to grab something to eat with me.

"Is there anything I can help you with?"

"Yes, you could go to my place and get me some clothes."

I frown, hoping she's not still in her wet clothes. "I thought Betsy brought you something to wear."

She groans loudly, and I listen as the bolt slides free. "If I open this door, do you promise not to laugh?"

What the hell is going on? "Yeah, I promise. I just want to make sure you're okay."

She swings the door open and, as I shine my light on her, my eyes drop to take in the very long, very big, and very ugly yellow daisy dress on her body. My jaw drops right along with my eyes.

"You promised not to laugh." She grabs the door about to swing it shut, but I snatch it and hold it open.

"I'm not laughing. I'm just..." I stop talking, unable to find the right words.

"Disturbed?"

Now I can't help but laugh, but it's okay, because Sawyer is laughing too. She pulls the oversized dress away from her body.

"What the hell is that?" I ask.

"I think it's called a house dress. Something elderly ladies wear for comfort. My late grandmother had the same one." I reach out and touch the fabric. "Polyester," she explains. "The real cheap kind."

I let the fabric go and it falls against her small body. "Okay, uh, just be sure not to stand too close to a candle. I think it might be flammable." That pulls another laugh from her and it wraps around me and squeezes my dick.

"I can't go out in public like this."

"Do you want to get back into your jeans?"

She bites her lip and shakes her head. "Then I'd hurt Betsy's feelings and I don't want to do that."

Thoughtful and adorable. "Want me to get food and bring it back?"

"No, I guess this will be okay."

I dip my head, meet her dark, unsettled eyes and smile. It's been a long time since I came across a girl who worried about hurting someone's feelings.

She angles her head. "Why are you smiling like that?"

"No reason. Look, it's just us. I think everyone else must be sleeping, besides you look good in daisies."

"Liar."

I could tell her she'd look great in a potato sack, but she wouldn't believe that either.

"Tomorrow, I'll hike back to your car and get your suitcase."

"No, that's ridiculous." She pulls the fabric out from her body again. "If I had my sewing kit..." She sighs and lets the fabric fall against her body. "I guess this will be fine for tonight." She sticks her head out and glances up and down the dark hall.

"The coast is clear," I tell her. She wraps her arms around herself, and that's when I realize it's pretty cool in the hallway. I peel off my sweatshirt and hand it to her. "Put this on. It will keep you warm and hide most of the dress and if Betsy sees you, she won't be offended."

"Won't you be cold?"

"No, I'm good."

She tugs on the sweater, which is also ten times too big for her, and smiles. "Thanks. If you get cold, let me know and I'll give it back."

I probably won't get cold while I'm hanging out with her, but I think it's best to keep that thought to myself. I nod and she glances into her room. "Let me grab my key." I shine the light on her and can't seem to tear my gaze away—house dress or not, she's beautiful—as she hurries to her dresser, and nearly trips on the hem of the long dress. She snatches up her key and locks up behind herself. We retrace our steps downstairs and find Betsy by the fire, her head tilted.

"I think she's asleep," I whisper and put my finger to my lips. We tiptoe through the main lodge and go down a long hall to the café. I shine my light around the empty space as Sawyer bumps into me from behind.

"It's kind of creepy," she murmurs, and curls her fingers into the back of my shirt. My protective instincts come out full force.

"I got you." I slow my steps and let her cling to me as I open a door that leads into the café. Her flashlight zooms around the place as she checks it out.

"Ohmigod," she shrieks, and I look to the left to see that we're reflected in a big glass door refrigerator.

I try not to laugh. I don't want to embarrass her. "That's just us, Sawyer. Come here." I twist and put my arm around her to hold her close.

"I feel like an idiot," she moans.

"You're not."

"I shouldn't watch so many scary movies." A chuckle bubbles out of her throat. "But I like them. When I'm at home, tucked in my bed."

The vision of Sawyer at home, tucked in her bed, in nothing but her 'underwear' trickles all the way to my dick and wakes it up again.

"How about we grab some sandwiches and eat them in my room?"

Did I just invite Sawyer to my motel room? It appears I did.

"Yeah, this kitchen is freaking me out. Let's hurry up."

I find a big fridge in the back, and shine my light on the contents. "Vegetarian? Vegan? Pescatarian?"

"I like meat." Her eyes go wide. "I mean..."

"How does ham and cheese sound?" I ask.

"That sounds gourmet right about now."

I chuckle and grab a few sandwiches and drinks, and Sawyer walks to another fridge and pulls out some things.

A loud crack goes through the room and Sawyer squeals. "What was that?" She steps close to me again.

"It's an old place and old places creak in the wind."

Our steps are quicker as we hurry from the kitchen and make our way back to the lobby, but when we do, Betsy is greeting another couple at the door.

"No, I'm sorry, we don't have any more rooms but you're more than welcome to hunker down here in the lobby. The fire is nice, and there's a sofa and a few chairs."

As Betsy shines the light on the couple, it occurs to me that they're elderly and no way can they sleep on that old sofa with their frail bones. I'm young and fit. The sofa might hurt my back, but it won't break it.

I glance at Sawyer, and she's frowning. She opens her mouth, but I call out, "They can have my room. I'll take the lobby."

"That's nice of you," Sawyer says. "I don't think you'll get much sleep, though."

"I don't have much choice. I can't let them sleep down here."

"Well, maybe you do have a choice..."

4

SAWYER

What on earth am I saying?

Shut your mouth, Sawyer, just shut it.

I don't know this guy. Sure, he picked me up and saved my ass before I froze to death, and sure I am ridiculously attracted to him—I even briefly considered a no strings hook-up—but really, offering up my room...my bed...to a guy I've only known for a few hours. That's so not like me. I must have hit my head on the steering wheel harder than I realized. Wait, nope. Can't blame it on that. The airbag prevented me from cracking my skull open and making bad decisions. If I can't blame it on a concussion, what can I blame it on?

An overactive libido?

Ah, yes, there's the answer I didn't want to admit.

"What are you suggesting?" he asks, as he juggles the sandwiches and drinks in his hands.

Yes, what exactly are you suggesting, Sawyer?

Let me think. One queen-sized bed. Two stranded people. Hot guy capable of deflowering a virgin. I shrug and try not to lose the two plates of pie in my hand as I struggle to appear casual.

"You'll have no privacy down here, and I mean there will be two of us in the room so that's no privacy either." Oh, boy, here I go rambling again. "I mean, you can take the bed and I'll camp out on the floor. Problem solved."

"Didn't you just tell me you didn't like camping?" He has such a cute smirk on his face I don't know whether to smack or kiss it off. "Sleeping on the ground wasn't for you?"

"Yes, well, your camping days consisted of a beachside villa, which clearly makes me the tougher one."

"I have no doubt you're tough, Sawyer."

I lift my chin an inch, liking the compliment. "Are we going to argue all day, or clear your room out and eat this food?"

"Yeah, I like your idea better."

"Oh, you are both such dears, but are you sure?" Betsy asks, once Chase and I stop arguing.

I nod and Chase says, "Positive. The bed is untouched, and I'll clear my things out. I'll drop the key on the dresser and leave the door open."

"Thank you so much," the elderly woman says, her voice tired and weary. "I hate to put you out, though."

"No worries, my friend here offered up her bed to me."

"That is so nice of you, Sawyer," Betsy says, and I can't see her face. She's old school, and is probably judging the hell out of me right now. I shouldn't care, but I'm always judged. I guess that's to be expected for a theater student—and daughter of an important sports coach.

"No problem," I say. Yes, it is nice of me and not at all altruistic. Okay, maybe a little.

I go up the stairs first and shine the light, and Chase follows behind. I wish my entire body wasn't so aware of him. Now I'm not even going to get a reprieve or be able to touch myself while thinking of him.

Oh God. Girl, get it together.

As we pass by the room before mine, and the door opens abruptly. I nearly jump out of my boots as I gasp, and press against Chase. Instinctively, I shine my light at the person who just popped out of the room.

"Oh, sorry," A guy around our age says and when he holds his hands up to block the light, I lower it. "Didn't mean to scare you." A pretty girl steps up beside him, shining her light on us, as she puts her arms around his waist. Her brow furrows a bit as she takes in my hideous dress, but she doesn't say anything so she's okay in my book.

"Hi there," she greets us, her voice light and cheery and friendly.

"Hi," both Chase and I say at the same time.

Her light swings from us to the man beside her. "I'm Danielle and this is Trev. Are you two snowed in too?"

"We are," I say.

She frowns. "Bummer."

"At least we're not one of the fifteen hundred stuck out on the Trans-Canada." Look at me putting a positive spin on things. Go Sawyer!

"We're trying to make the best of it, too," she tells us and snuggles in tighter to Trev. "We were actually on our way to the airport for our honeymoon." She holds her ring finger out. "Newlyweds."

"Congratulations." I lean forward to admire her ring in the dark. Who the hell gets married this time of year? Then again, who am I to judge? They clearly had their reasons.

Trev laughs. "We're on our way to the café for sustenance." He nudges Chase. "If you know what I mean." His gaze goes to the food in our hands, and he laughs harder. "Of course, you know what I mean. You two are already fueling up for a long night."

"We're not—" I shake my head and glance at Chase, who doesn't seem in a hurry to tell them we're not together.

Noise on the stairs echo behind us as the elderly couple heads to Chase's room. "We'd better go," I say to Chase, and nod toward the room.

"Yeah, you better," Trev says playfully and tugs his door shut. The two of them giggle as they head down the hall and I'm happy they're making the best of their time. I sigh as I watch them go. That's the kind of love I want, and doubt I'll ever have.

"That's sweet," I say, my voice wistful.

"Now right there. That's two people with their glass half full."

What is it with Chase and his glasses? I don't know but I nod in agreement. "Good for them."

I walk to my room and jiggle the lock open, trying not to be envious of the newlyweds. Chase follows me in and deposits all the food onto the small table, and heads back to his room to get his things. A few minutes later, he drops a bag onto my floor, and I don't miss the way his big body seems to eat up all the room.

It's going to be a long ass night.

I snatch up a sandwich and soft drink and sit cross-legged on the bed, pulling the god-awful house dress over my legs so I don't flash him. We've talked about my underwear enough today. I move back against the headboard and the springs squeak. I'm sure the mattress must be from the eighteen hundreds. Okay, I'm exaggerating but my brain is spinning out of control as Chase moves around the room, grabbing a hanger from the closet and putting his damp coat up next to mine. Once done, he pulls the rickety chair out from the desk and sits on it.

"Whoa," he says as it wobbles.

"You're going to break it. You're too big." I pat the bed like the idiot I am. "Bring the food and come sit here."

He kicks off his boots and joins me on the bed, sitting cross-legged and facing me. "I'm starving," I say for lack of anything else.

"Getting stranded in a snowstorm will do that to you."

I peel the plastic off the sandwich and take a big bite. "I used to be vegetarian. For about a week," I tell him, simply to make conversation.

He cracks his drink and takes a big gulp. "Oh, yeah," he says when he's done. "What happened?"

"A big juicy burger."

He takes a bite of his sandwich and laughs. "Hard to resist a big juicy burger."

"Juicy meat is my jam."

Wait, did that sound weird? Sexual? Not that I'm good at sex talk or anything. I'm a walking, talking virgin, partly because the guys at the academy are too afraid to look at me—thanks Dad—and partly because I'll always be that chubby girl that continually gets overlooked. Although, this guy doesn't know I'm hands off, the boring drama queen. Not that I'm a *drama* queen. I just mean, I'm a theater major at the academy. I seriously have no drama. How could I? There isn't a guy on campus that pays me an iota of attention. Chase doesn't know that though, and from the way he's looking at me, I think he likes what he sees. Maybe while we're snowed in, he doesn't have to know I'm boring, hands-off Sawyer, the coach's daughter.

The whole point of going to Florida was to be who I wanted to be. A girl with no history or baggage. A girl who could finally get rid of her pesky virginity.

"Did you get a hold of your friend?" he asks.

"Yes, and I called home, how about you?"

"I let everyone know." He swallows another big bite. "You think it could be days, huh?"

"Sorry, but yes."

He glances around the dark room. "What the hell are we going to do with ourselves for days without power?"

Oh, I could think of a few things, but I keep my mouth shut and just shrug.

"Betsy said she had a generator. Maybe I could look at it tomorrow."

"You know how to work a generator?"

"My dad is handy and I'm pretty good with my hands."

My gaze goes directly to his big, sturdy hands and I'm so glad it's dark and he can't see the shiver that just went through me. Maybe he felt it, though. Maybe it reverberated through the bed. Would it be terrible if he knew I was attracted to him? I mean, I do want a no strings hook-up, and after a few days at the motel, chances are I'll never see him again.

"What do you do for fun in Nova Scotia?"

I crack my drink and take a sip, hoping it will cool my body. My room is actually chilly, but if I keep thinking about sex, I'm sure it will warm me through the night. "I curl."

"Curl what?"

I laugh and whack him, and holy hell when my hand hits with hard man chest, I nearly choke on my sandwich. I finally swallow it. "Curling, you know..." I mimic throwing a rock, but this guy is American and probably has no idea what curling is.

He laughs. "I know what curling is. I was just messing with you." He glances at the window. "Hey if we're stuck for days, maybe we can find a pond."

"I don't have my rocks in my back pocket."

"Of course not, those things are heavy."

"You've played?"

"No, but I love all sports."

"I hate hockey," I blurt out, and he stiffens.

"Jeez, what did hockey ever do to you?"

"Let's just say I hate everything about it."

"Including the players?"

I snort and don't bother telling him it's not the sport itself I hate, but the players. I guess he's smart enough to figure that out by my reaction though.

"What kind of a Canadian are you?"

"I just had a bad experience," is all I say. If I'm pretending to be someone I'm not, I can't tell him who my dad is and how he subtly, or not so subtly, lets his players know I'm off limits. Maybe I should move to Boston. Why I thought it was a great idea to go to the academy where my dad coaches is beyond me. Well, okay I know why and it's because it has the top theater program in Canada.

Seriously though, hockey players are egotistical jerks. Over the years I've heard about the locker room teasing, the laying down of bets on who can bag the most girls each season. One day I happened to walk into the locker room looking for my father. I thought the team was still on the ice practicing. Little did I know they were talking about me, and taking bets on who could pop my cherry. God, it was a nightmare come true. I remember being frozen in my tracks, hidden behind a string of lockers, horrified and trying not to cry as they talked about me like I was nothing but a piece of meat.

A few guys took the bet, but in the end, they must have chickened out. No one dared to ask me out, and I'm not convinced it's because they were afraid of their coach, who's my dad. Don't get me started on their antics when they're at an away game. They screw anything with two legs, even if they have girlfriends back home. Ugh.

A loud cracking noise goes through the walls again and I nearly jump off the bed. "What was that?"

"Just the wind," he assures me, but I'm not convinced.

"Do you think this place is haunted?"

I hold my flashlight up, and he winces. "No, and can you shine that somewhere else."

"I think it's haunted," I tell him.

"Then it's a good thing I'm sharing your room." He reaches out and squeezes my bicep. "You'll be able to protect me with these strong curling muscles."

He's joking, I think, but I am strong, and I like that he knows it. I finish my sandwich and unwrap a slice of pie. "Shoot, I didn't grab any forks."

"Eat it with your fingers. That's what I plan to do." He picks up his pie on the small plate. "I'm so glad you grabbed these, they look delicious."

"I don't know what kind they are."

"It's pie, who cares."

"Exactly what was I thinking." I push the pie until it's hanging off the edge of my plate and bite into it. "Mmm, apple."

He breaks a big piece off with his hand and tosses the dripping mess into his mouth. His eyes briefly close, like he's having a moment, and then they spring open. "Mmm, cherry, my favorite." He picks the piece of pie up, not caring at all that cherries are dripping out, and positions the plate under it as he holds it out for me. I take a big bite and it spills down my chin.

"That is so good," I moan as I chew.

"Right?"

He bites into it again, and the next thing I know he runs his finger along my chin to clean up the mess. He doesn't wipe his hand clean, though. Nope, instead he brings it to his mouth to lick clean, and I swear to God, I lose every ounce of breath in my lungs as I watch him. I struggle to breathe, but involuntary body functions are a thing of the past as arousal fries my brain cells.

"Want another bite?" he asks.

I work to recover my voice. "No, I'm good." Jeez I hate that I sound like a damn chipmunk, and really, I don't want to take another bite away from him when he's enjoying it so much.

There's hope in his eyes when he asks, "Do you know if there were any more slices?"

"I don't know, I just grabbed two and had no idea what they were."

"I'd better eat it slow then."

"Yeah, slow...slow is good." My god, he's practically making love to that pie. What must he be like in bed? Would he take his time to savor the girl, the same as he's doing with that slice of pie? Oh, God, it's crazy how much I want to find out.

I wipe my brow with the back of my hand. "You ah, you really like cherry, huh?"

"It's only my favorite."

I swallow, and work my best not to put a sexual spin on this but my attempts are futile. That's right, everything about this guy makes me think of sex, and now tonight, when I'm all tucked in, I'm going to be thinking about how much he likes cherries, and how I have one that's completely intact, and it's his for the taking.

5

CHASE

Why is Sawyer's face all twisted up as she looks at me? Do I have pie all over my cheeks or something? No, probably not. She's probably looking at me like I'm a weirdo for making bedroom noises as I eat. But it's not my fault the pie is delicious. It likely is my fault that I'm making a big ravenous fool of myself, though. Oh well. I shove the last piece of crust into my mouth and check my watch. It's only eight, but with no lights, no books and no power—and after the tiring day we had—maybe we should just get some sleep.

"Do you think they have running water?"

"They're probably on town water, so yeah. At least I hope they are."

I hold my sticky fingers up. "I need to wash up."

I'm about to push off the bed when she says, "Licking them wasn't working?" I stop and glance at her as the flashlight casts shadows on her pretty face.

"Was I that disgusting?" I laugh. "My mom taught me better than that."

"I...didn't mind," she responds, her voice sounding a little higher, and maybe a little broken. I resist the urge to pick the flashlight up and shine it right in her eyes. Did she like watching me lick my fingers? Did it make her think about other things...like me licking her?

My dick jumps in my pants, and as I gaze at her, once again taking in her innocence, I shake my head. Clearly lack of sex is getting to me, kicking my imagination into hyperdrive and I'm the only one with the dirty mind here. But seriously though, can she be as innocent as she seems?

I push to my feet. "Hey, we gotta do what we gotta do when roughing it," I finally answer as she sits on the bed blinking at me.

"Right, so let me make a bed on the floor." She jumps up but before she can grab blankets, I capture her wrist. I don't miss the fast intake of air. I let her go. "I'm sorry, I shouldn't have...I was just trying to stop you. I am not letting you take the floor."

"I don't want you to have to sleep on it either."

"How about a pillow wall?"

She angles her head, and crinkles her nose. "A what?"

I laugh at that. "You know, we put pillows in between us...on the bed. When I was a kid and we all wanted to have a sleep-over at the cottage, and I bunked with Daisy, or Khloe, or Amelia, we used pillows to separate us." Speaking of Daisy, she's at Scotia Academy, playing hockey on the girls' team. I was hoping to see her this week, too.

"You've slept with a lot of girls."

"No, I mean, well...Okay no, we were all kids. Their parents were friends of my parents, and we all vacationed together. I also made a pillow wall with my buddy Brandon, and the other guys."

"I've never made a pillow wall...My girlfriends and I just slept together." As if realizing how that might sound, she quickly adds, "Not like that. But as friends. I...like guys."

"I like girls," I say, and I think guys are just weird when it comes to sharing a bed with another guy. She turns and looks at the bed, and goes quiet. "I really don't mind taking the floor, Sawyer."

"No, that's stupid."

"It wasn't stupid when you were going to do it."

She grins. "No, it's only stupid when you were going to."

I shake my head at that logic, but we're both so tired, I'm not sure after the big adrenaline dump that either of us know what we're saying. She takes a deep breath and when she lets it out, it's clear she's warming to the idea of sharing, and you know what, I'm not sure it's a good idea. Maybe I'd be better off sleeping in my car. Maybe that will cool me down and freeze out all my sexual thoughts.

She puts her hands on her hips and nods. "It does seem like a logical solution."

Ah yes, logic. I might be a bit short on that tonight. I hold my sticky fingers up. "I promise to keep these on my side."

Unless of course, she doesn't want me to.

Cut it out, dude!

She holds her hand out to shake on it. "Deal."

I keep my hands at my sides. "It will have to be an oral deal."

"What?" she asks, her eyes growing big.

"My hands are sticky. I don't want to get you dirty, so our bedroom deal will have to just be an oral arrangement."

"Oh, you mean a verbal agreement."

"Yeah, that's what I mean." *Jesus, Chase get it together.* Why would I say oral when I meant verbal? Oh, probably because I'm about to crawl into bed with a beautiful woman, and I can't help but want to put my mouth all over her. But there will be no oral sex, no oral anything tonight, and the only thing going into my mouth is my toothbrush. "Let me check for running water."

Needing a moment to get my shit together, I practically run to the bathroom and try the taps. "They work," I call over my shoulder, but Sawyer is standing right there.

She laughs. "Good thing we made that verbal agreement before I went deaf."

"Sorry about that." I rip the paper off a bar of soap and wash up.

"I don't even have my toothbrush."

"Mine is new, you can use it. I can run downstairs and see if they have any spare ones."

"I can run down."

"Are we doing this again?" I ask.

She laughs. "I'm too tired to argue." She glances over her shoulder when the wind howls and what sounds like a loose shingle overhead bangs against the roof. God, she really is scared. I rub my hand on her arm to soothe her. "Can you...hurry?"

"I'll be fast, but if you want, you can come with me, or I can just use mouthwash tonight."

She puts her hand on my chest. "No, you should go. Just hurry. But not too fast. I don't want you to fall down the stairs or get hurt in the dark."

"Aww, are you worried about me, Sawyer?" I tease.

"It's kind of all about me. If you fall and break your neck, then I'll be all alone, and this place is haunted." I'm about to tell her it's just her imagination, when a big bang on the roof practically reverberates through my body.

"That came from the ceiling," she shrieks and snuggles into me.

"Come on." I walk her backward, pull down the blankets and gesture for her to get in. "Stay right here until I get back." I pull the sheets up to her chin, and she nods. "You need to stop watching scary movies."

"I like them..." I arch my brow and her lips turn up at the corners. "Until I'm alone after dark."

I laugh. "Okay, I'll be right back, and I'll lock up after I leave."

"But what if the ghost is already inside?"

"You're tough, remember," I remind her and nudge her chin with my fist. "Knock him out with the lamp."

She gives me a look that suggests I might be insane. "That will go right through a ghost."

"You're killing me, Sawyer," I say and bite back a laugh. God, she's so damn adorable, but I don't want her to be frightened. "Think about how nice Florida is going to be when you get there. When I get back you can tell me all the fun things you had planned." She stifles a yawn. "If you're still awake, that is."

With the flashlight leading the way, I hurry to the door and take a fast glance back at her. She's holding the sheets to her chin, her gaze latched on me. I leave the room and lock the door tightly behind me. The hall is quiet and dark as I make my way to the front lobby, where I find Betsy behind the counter. I'm surprised she's still up. I ask about toiletries, and she fills me up with shampoo, a toothbrush and toothpaste and even a comb. I let her know I can take a look at the generator tomorrow if she'd like and she brightens up. Just as I'm about to leave, she hands me a bottle of wine to thank me for giving up my room and I can't help but think a glass might take the edge off for Sawyer and help her sleep.

I hurry back to the room, and as I walk down the hall and hear creaking noises, I have to admit, the place is kind of creepy. I glance over my shoulder as I quickly open the door, step inside and lock it behind myself.

"It's me," I call out as I enter and try not to sound as unsettled as I feel. I glance around but she's gone. "Sawyer?" I try not to panic. Could this place be haunted, could she be—

That thought evaporates as the bathroom door creaks open. "I'm here," she announces as she wipes toothpaste from her mouth. "Nature called and I couldn't wait. I brushed up while I was in there."

I laugh, and tell her, "I got everything and Betsy hooked me up with a bottle of wine. A thank you for giving up my room." I shine the light on it. "Want a glass?"

"Yup," she says and sits on the bed, and I can't help but think after we finish it, we could play spin the bottle which is a ridiculous idea, and not just because there are only two of us. She hugs herself as a chill goes through her.

"Do you think our coats are dry enough to wear?" I walk to the closet and check, but they're still damp. "Nope. Afraid not."

"Let's just wrap up in the blankets."

"Good idea." I grab two water glasses from the bathroom, and take them and the bottle of the wine to bed. I twist the cap off.

"Oh, the fancy stuff," she teases.

"Guaranteed to knock you off your ass and put you to sleep."

Wind howls outside as she shakes a blanket out and hands it to me. "I'm actually okay with that tonight."

I drape the blanket over myself and get comfortable on the bed, and she does the same beside me. I carefully pour us each a glass and we hold them out in salute. "What should we toast to?"

"To not being stuck on the Trans-Canada and to hoping all those who are, are staying warm and not starving."

"I'll drink to that," I agree.

"And to not dying when I crashed my car."

I grin. "I'll drink to that too."

"And to having someone nice rescue me, and keep me company."

"And again, I'll drink to that." After three drinks, our glasses are almost empty, so I refill them.

"I'm a bit of a lightweight," she admits.

"That's okay. No one has to drive and you're safe with me." I take a drink and tease, "But am I safe with you?"

She laughs, and holds one hand up like she's going to slam it into my airpipe. "Judo," she says.

"Where did you learn judo?"

"A friend."

"Oh yeah."

"She also taught me some other words in Japanese."

I stare at her for a second as her lips quiver, like she's holding back a laugh. "Jesus," I say, when I finally clue in. "Funny girl."

"It worked, didn't it? It stopped you from wanting to mess with me."

"Well..." I can't help but think about all the ways we could mess around. "I don't know about that."

She eyes me. "Don't know about what?"

"Let's just say this, judo or not, I'd never hurt you or do anything you didn't want to do. You can trust me on that."

She angles her head and her nose crinkles up. "But you want to mess with me?"

I take a drink to stifle my moan as I remind myself of her innocence. "I think 'messing' with you can be interpreted in numerous ways."

She frowns for a second and looks into her glass of wine. Her head lifts abruptly, and she says, "Oh, you mean..."

"Sawyer, you're a beautiful woman, and I'm a guy. Let's just leave it at that, and a pillow wall between us. Not that I'd take advantage of you in any way, but if I feel your body against mine, it might do things to my body that I have no control over and it's probably best if that doesn't happen."

"Oh, okay."

"Besides, I'm sure you have a boyfriend back home."

"I don't."

"Really? I find that hard to believe."

"I don't lie. Guys just aren't...anyway..." She lets her words fall off, and I'm about to press when she asks, "Do you have someone?"

"No, I don't have a boyfriend or a girlfriend."

"I find that hard to believe," she says shooting my words back at me.

"I've been busy."

"You've never been in a serious relationship with someone?"

"Nope." I've never made time for a serious partner. Sex is one thing, but planning a future with someone is something else entirely. There's just been so much pressure on me to succeed, that I didn't have time for one more thing. I can only concentrate on the here and now.

"What have you been busy with?" she asks.

I shrug. "School, other things..."

Needing to change the subject—I don't really want to tell her who I am and ruin this nice, intimate moment, heck she already said she hates hockey, and probably the players too—I pour more wine into our glasses and say, "I guess telling ghost stories in the dark is out. That's what we used to do around the bonfires when we were kids."

"We could play the drinking game Never Have I Ever."

I laugh. "I haven't played that in years."

She holds her glass up. "I'm just working with what we have, Chase." I nod, and get the sense that this sweet girl has no idea what she's working with. I haven't known her long but she's sweet, and sexy and innocent and funny. Hard not to like a girl with those traits.

Don't think about hard.

"Okay, I'll go first," I say, and swirl the wine in my glass as I glance at the half empty bottle beside me. "Never have I ever played spin the bottle."

She takes a drink and I laugh. "That was an easy one." Her gaze goes to the bottle. "Wait, is that something you want to do?"

I shrug. "Hard to do with just two people."

There's that word hard again.

"Okay, never have I ever mooned someone." She starts laughing when I take a drink. "Are you serious?"

"Ah, yeah, let's move on." She continues to laugh and I'm thinking the wine is already getting to her. "Okay, never have I ever had a random hook-up."

I take a drink but she doesn't. "That's kind of what I planned to do in Florida." As soon as the words leave her mouth, her jaw drops open and her eyes go wide. "I mean..."

"Hey, it's okay. If you want to have a random hook-up, there's nothing wrong with it. I'm not here to judge."

She relaxes a bit. "Thanks."

"But you'll be safe, right?"

"Yes, Dad," she groans with a laugh.

"So, your dad knows you're going to Florida for a hook-up?"

"No!"

"Of course not. What am I even saying?" I divide the last of the wine between us and hope come morning she's not embarrassed by this conversation. "Want to keep playing?"

She closes one eye in thought. "Never have I ever gone skinny dipping." Again, I drink, and it makes her laugh. "Is there anything you haven't done?"

I wave my finger back and forth. "Not your turn." Since she's still going down a sexual path, I ask, "Never have I ever had sex."

She lifts her drink, and holds it near her mouth as her eyes meet mine. Our gazes lock, and her hand is perfectly still for a second. I'm smart enough to realize she's debating on whether she wants to tell me the truth or not. "No judgement," I murmur quietly. She nods and sets her glass down.

The room spins around me. How the hell is she still a virgin? Is it a religious thing or something, because damn, I wanted her the second she removed her hood and blinked at me.

"Guilty," she says, and an embarrassed groan crawls out of her throat.

"There's nothing wrong with being a virgin," I tell her. "Is it a religious thing?"

This brings on a hysterical laugh. "No, it's a guy thing." I stare at her, not really sure what she means. She finishes off the wine in her glass. "You might as well know that I've played spin the bottle, but it never landed on me. I was pretty sure it did this one time, but Jaxon nudged it, just so he didn't have to kiss me."

I take her glass from her and set both of ours on the night-stand. "Jaxon's a fucking moron."

She starts laughing and I snatch up the bottle and spin it. It gets caught up in the blanket wrapped around her body and doesn't land on her, and her shoulders sag as she lets out a breath. I nudge the bottle until it's pointing directly at her, and she draws her bottom lip between her teeth, her gaze slowly lifts to mine.

"Chase?"

"Looks like it's pointing right at you, Sawyer." She swallows and it can be heard over the blowing wind. "Can I kiss you?"

"You sort of have to. The bottle...I mean...it..."

I lean forward and swallow whatever it is she's trying to say to me. Her soft lips part, become pliable against my mouth, and I moan and place my palm on her cheek. She leans into me, a little noise catching in her throat and my synapses fire so quick, I'm sure my brain is going to explode. Never in my life have I kissed a girl like her, and the taste of her innocence is fucking with me big time—in a good way.

We stay like that as the wind howls outside, my heart hammers in my chest, and my cock jumps to life, encouraging me to take this further, but I can't. She's an innocent and she's been drinking and while I might have a swollen dick, I am not a dick.

I slowly break the kiss and stare at her. Her eyes are still closed, and her lips are poised for me. "Sawyer," I whisper softly. Her lids open and she sits up a bit straighter. Her fingers go to her lips and I can't help but wonder if they're as tingly as mine.

I pick up the empty bottle. "We, uh…"

"You hated it," she blurts out.

"What…no."

She shakes her head like she doesn't believe me. "It's getting late. We should go to bed." I can't see well in the dark, but I'm sure her cheeks are turning a shade darker. She begins to scramble away, but I don't want her to be embarrassed by any of this. I capture her arm, and hold her still.

"For the record, that was really nice," I say.

"Chase—" she begins.

"In fact, I liked it so much, I'd like to kiss you more…" For one split second, I debate on telling her what's on my mind, but she's been honest with me, so I tell her, "Kiss you all over."

She gasps, but I don't miss her smile.

"Really?"

"I have no reason to lie. You're gorgeous, Sawyer, but you've been drinking and right now, it's a bad idea."

She nods, but smiles. "Okay."

Jeez, she could have put up a little bit of a fight. What am I saying? I wouldn't take her tonight if she begged me. Well, maybe if she begged me.

Get it together, Chase.

I gesture toward the bathroom. "I need to brush up."

"I should again too."

"You want to go first?"

She grabs her flashlight, and I shine mine on her as she hops from the bed and stumbles just a little on the dress as she gathers up the supplies I brought and makes her way into the bathroom. Man, she really is a lightweight. I lay back, arms behind my head, and work to get my dick under control as she washes and brushes up for bed. It's insane to think how my plans have veered off course so much, and while I'd never admit it to anyone, I'm not disappointed. I like being here with Sawyer.

She finally comes out of the bathroom, and I take my turn to wash up, and as I walk back to the bed, I find two pillows running the length of it.

"I found these in the closet."

"Great."

"I uh...I'm kind of glad you're staying in my room."

"Same," I say, because I'm clearly a masochist. My cock has been up and down more than the stock market, and that's saying something.

I walk to the empty side of the bed, turn off my flashlight and set it on the nightstand. "I'll sleep in my jeans, but are you okay if I take my T-shirt off?"

"Sure."

I tug it over my head and slide between the heavy bedding. I stretch out my weary bones, being careful to keep my arms and legs on my side of the pillows. I take deep breaths to quiet my body and mind, as I listen to her soft breathing noises. I suspect she's lying awake over there, pretending to be asleep. Are her thoughts running down the same path as mine? She did say she wanted a random hook-up when she was in Florida. No. No. No. We've been drinking and I'm not about to take advantage of her or the situation.

I close my eyes and will sleep to come. My cock is finally settled and I'm seconds from drifting off, but jolt awake at the sound of moans and groans filling the quiet of the night. My lids fly open, and I concentrate on the sound. The second I realize what's going on my dick decides it's time to wake up again.,

"Chase," Sawyer says, her voice quiet, and shaky. She's obviously terrified.

"It's okay. Go to sleep," I say, my throat tight as my stupid dick continues to swell.

"Sleep? How am I supposed to sleep? Don't you hear all those moans and groans?"

"I do." She shimmies closer, and I pull one of the pillows to me, to keep her from accidently feeling my hard cock. I jump when a loud bang reverberates through our wall and she yelps.

"Did you hear that bang?"

"I heard it."

She spins my way, and I can barely see her face in the dark. "I told you this place was haunted."

"Um, Sawyer, that's our neighbors."

"What?"

"That's Danielle and Trev, next door. They're ah..." The headboard hits our adjoining wall, and our bed practically vibrates. "Banging."

"Ohmigod."

"Yeah, they're singing praise to God, too."

She starts laughing and reaches between us to grab a pillow against my body. She puts it over her head to muffle the noise, and the pillow near our feet falls over the end of the bed as it jiggles. Great, now there's nothing separating us but her house dress and my jeans.

"Shh," I say, and pull her to me. "They're going to hear you."

"So, this place isn't haunted," she states, her voice low and hard to hear with the pillow over her face.

"I don't know about that, but those noises are definitely coming from the newlyweds next door."

Her warm body vibrates against me and I hold my breath. If she moves one more inch my way, she's in for a real surprise. As she laughs, she shimmies my way and her sweet backside brushes against my unapologetic erection—traitorous prick that he is. I know the instant she realizes what's going on beneath the sheets. Her entire body stops moving, and I'm not even certain she's still breathing.

"Chase?"

"Yeah?"

"Was that..."

6

SAWYER

I don't bother finishing my sentence, where I planned to jokingly ask him if he brought the flashlight to bed. Not only is it no joke, I wouldn't be able to verbalize the words even if I wanted to. Not with the way my throat is drying up, and my voice is choked out by the heat zinging through me.

Chase has an erection, a big, hard, mouth-watering erection.

Mouth-watering?

Good Lord, I've clearly had too much wine and my libido is running rampant as inhibitions fade into the background. And don't even get me started on that kiss. No man has ever kissed me like that before. Okay, to be fair, I don't have anything to compare it to other than what I've read in books and watched on TV. Nevertheless, it was hot, exciting, and stirred things in me that I never even knew existed.

Wait! Did he say he'd take me if I wasn't drinking?

Ohmigod he did, which means no alcohol shall pass these lips again—for as long as we're stuck here, that is.

He called you gorgeous.

My heart beats a bit faster as I stare at him, and his face twists, like he's trying to figure out the right answer to my question.

"We should sleep," I say, wanting to cut him some slack and end his torment for now. Tomorrow however, when we're both sober, I might do everything I can to tease and taunt him, because yeah, I wouldn't mind it one little bit if this guy was my first. From his erection, I'm guessing under the right circumstances he'd be game. Seriously though, he finds me attractive?

I almost snort out a laugh. Without knowing my history, that I was a chubby teen and now I'm a drama nerd—on no man's radar—he's only judging me on what he sees, and I kind of like that. Why should we let our pasts cloud our judgements? Then again, he could just be super aroused because our neighbors are having loud sex. Maybe the sound is simply stirring and elevating his arousal and I'm the only female around.

Since I'm desperate to get rid of my virginity, I'll take it!

"Yeah, sleep," he agrees, his voice rough and labored as he jumps from the bed to grab the pillow that had fallen off. I stuff the other one between us and move all the way to the edge. I turn my back to him and curl up, willing sleep to come as the neighbours continue to bang their headboard on the wall.

"How long does it—"

"Christ," he responds before I can finish.

I very carefully turn and find him on his side staring at me. I punch my pillow to flatten it so I can see his face. He does the same. "I was just curious."

"It's different for everyone, and different each time."

"How so?"

His face twists, like he's in pain, and maybe he is. "It's just... okay...well, if a guy is drinking, it could take longer, or he could get whiskey dick."

"Whiskey dick?"

"He can't get it up." He holds his hand up, index finger out and makes a deflating sound as he lets his finger fall toward the bed.

"I don't think Trev had any whiskey." I cover my mouth as I chuckle. "Has that ever happened to you?"

"No."

"You've never had any trouble getting it up?"

"Are we really having this conversation, Sawyer?"

Is he...blushing? "Sorry, I was just wondering." I'm about to turn back over, but he reaches out and puts his hand on my arm.

"It's okay. If you want to know, I'll answer as best I can."

What I really want to know is this: why does his touch feel so good, and why do I feel it all the way through my body, especially deep between my legs?

"Thank you."

He takes a fast, harsh breath, lets it out, and his brow furrows. I'm guessing he's trying to find the best way to explain this to me. I'm not a total idiot. I might be a virgin, but there are things I know about a woman's body. A guy's body, not so much, and I'm a bit fascinated.

"If a man is really, really aroused, because he's really into the girl he's with, it might only take minutes before he ejaculates. Some guys use tricks to stay hard so they don't orgasm too fast."

"Why would they do that?" I ask.

"Some want their partner to come first."

"Do you?"

"Yes. Always."

"I think that's admirable." I don't have restless leg syndrome, but I suddenly can't keep my legs or my body still. I shift an inch closer until his scent reaches my nose. "What kind of tricks do guys use?"

He shakes his head, his lips pinched tight like he's trying not to laugh. "I was afraid you were going to ask that."

I smile.

"You don't have to answer if you don't want."

"I don't want to but I'm going to answer anyway. They think of other things, other than the pleasure. Like maybe math or..." He gestures toward the window. "Like how they nearly went off the road in a bad blizzard or something."

I smile at that. Is he thinking of the blizzard to get his current erection under control? "I don't think I'd want a guy thinking about math or anything else if we were having sex. It seems...mechanical, less intimate. Do you know what I mean?"

He laughs, hard. "Don't worry, Sawyer. When a guy has sex with you, he won't be thinking about anything but you."

"You don't know that."

"Let's just say I know from experience."

"Are you very experienced? If you don't mind me asking. I know you said you've never been serious, but sex and love are two different things."

I honestly can't believe the direction of our conversation, but I'm curious and I feel safe with him, and how can we not talk or think about sex with the banging going on next door.

"Yeah, I've been with a lot of girls over the years."

"I like that you're honest."

He frowns and glances down. What, is he not being honest with me? What's going on in that head of his?

"I just...haven't been with anyone in a while," he admits.

"Ah, is that why you have..." I gesture toward his nether regions. "...You know."

"An erection?"

"Yeah."

"We're talking about sex, and I'm answering all your questions and you can't even say erection."

"I can say it."

"Then say it?" I take in his dimple as he smiles.

"Erection," I blurt out. "You like dirty talk, Chase?"

He rolls to his back and laughs, and for a brief second I feel stupid for asking the question.

"First, saying the word erection isn't dirty talk. Or at least I didn't think it was until you said it, and now, I can't ever unhear it and will probably lay here all night with a painful erection with no way to take care of it."

"Erection," I say again, just to play with him.

He curses under his breath. "If you know what's good for you, Sawyer, you'll stop saying that."

"What would happen if I didn't?" Okay, now I'm getting brazen and yes, I have to blame it on the alcohol because this is completely out of character for me.

"I'd probably pull you under me and fuck you with my *erection*, but like I said, we've been drinking, so I won't."

Bang. Bang. Bang.

"You could show it to me though, right?" What the hell? Did I really just say that?

His entire body stiffens. "Are you fucking serious?"

"I mean, I don't want you laying here in pain all night." I crinkle my face like I'd just sucked on a lemon.

"It's not painful, it's uncomfortable."

"Okay, uncomfortable then."

He stares at me, like he's trying to figure out if I'm messing with him or not. "I'm not going to lay here and get off in front of you."

"I can help."

He sits up, his feet over the side of the bed, his back to me as he rakes restless fingers through his hair and once again, I visualize those hands on my body.

"Would it make it easier if I touched myself?"

He shifts on the bed his dark, hungry eyes latching on me. "You do that?"

"I'm a virgin, but I'm still a girl with urges. I like to touch myself."

"Why are you a virgin, Sawyer?" His voice is pained and strained as he asks that. "If you're holding out for someone special, it's not me."

"It's not that. Like you, I've been very busy. I have school, and theater, and curling."

"Earlier you said it was a guy thing. I can't believe guys aren't all over you." He frowns and looks down. "Did someone hurt you?"

"No," I say. "Not in the way you're implying, not physically, I mean." The guys in the locker room hurt my feelings sure, but that's not what he's talking about. "The timing has never been right and well, the opportunity just hasn't..." I shift, to try to see his erection, and be funny when I say, "Arisen."

He shakes his head and laughs at my bad joke. "I want to touch you," he murmurs quietly.

"I want you to touch me too," I admit. I sit up and push the blankets off me. My ridiculous house dress is high on my legs, barely covering my panties. He groans as his focus turns to my thighs, and I have no idea how to tease, but I slowly inch them open. Correction: I know how to tease, judging by the loud rumble rising in his throat.

"You are so hot," he grumbles as I take in the way his cock is straining against his jeans.

"That looks like it hurts."

He reaches for his button and stops. "Are you sure?"

"Positive," I say, my pulse jumping in anticipation. "I really want to see you."

"I won't fuck you, Sawyer. Not when you've been drinking, but if you're really curious, then this..." he says, glancing at his cock. His gaze moves to my upper thighs. "And that. There are things we can do that can make us both feel good."

"Oral things, like you were talking about earlier?"

"Yeah, oral, and the reason that slipped out was because ever since I set eyes on you, I wanted my mouth on you."

My nipples swell, and poke against the thin dress. He groans as his gaze moves to them. I arch forward, offering myself to him. "Yes, please."

He swallows hard, and his brow furrows like he's still not sure, but I'm sure. I want this. I want him.

"No regrets come morning?" he asks and I honestly love how he's worried about me. "We might be stuck in this room for a while, and I couldn't live with myself if I did something you didn't really want, and hated me for it."

"No regrets. I want this. This is exactly what I was hoping to do in Florida, and since I can't get to Florida, you're the next best thing."

He angles his head. "I'm what?"

I chuckle. "I think that came out all wrong. You're better than the next best thing. You *are* the best thing."

"You're looking for a one night, no strings hook-up?"

"Yes, and I only want that with you."

"Because I'm the only guy your age in this motel?"

"No, because you're fucking hot." My pulse leaps. I can't believe the things I'm saying to this guy, but I'm never going to set eyes on him again, so why not be completely honest?

"You're fucking hot too, Sawyer."

With that, he stands, rips into his button and the hiss of his zipper travels all the way down my spine. I go up on my knees, my dress falling to the bed, and shimmy a bit closer. He shoves his jeans and boxers to his knees, and I gasp a little as his cock springs free. My gaze goes to his and I grin.

"Like what you see, Sawyer?" I nod and he grips the base of his cock, groaning as he strokes his long length. Precum pools on his tip and without thought, I reach out and run my finger through it, massaging it over his swollen crown.

"Fuck."

"You okay?"

His eyes roll back in his head. "That feels fucking good."

"I'm doing it right?"

"You're doing everything right."

I shift, and set myself on the edge of the bed, my feet on the floor. With his cock only inches from my face, I lean forward and lick the cum I swirled around his head. I savor the tangy flavor, and as more drips from his slit and he curses under his breath, it urges me on. I lap at him, and one of his hands goes to my hair, his fingers curling in my locks as his other hand continues to stroke his cock. I watch and learn and can't believe how much I love this. Something about his moans, the pleasure he's taking from my mouth, boosts my ego and fills me with a sense of empowerment.

"Sawyer," he moans. "Jesus, you're killing me."

His other hand moves my hair from my face and I angle my head to see if he's watching me. I place my hands on his cock as I slide him to the back of my throat. I go still for a quick second, as I'm about to gag, but once I get that under control, I resume the motion, riding him with my mouth. He sways as I take him deeper, and I slide my hand lower to touch his balls. He gasps, and thickens even more in my mouth, and I suddenly feel like I might have bitten off more than I can chew because if he lets go and comes, do I swallow or spit it out?

The next thing I know, his hands are on my shoulders and he's pushing me off his dick. I blink up at him, my heart stalling. Did I do something wrong?

"I'm too close." I stare at him, unsure, and he explains. "I need to taste your pussy. I want you to come first, all over my mouth."

Oh my God, I love how he talks.

I try to sound casual, although I'm anything but. "Oh, okay."

He puts his arm around me and in one fast, fluid movement, he has me flat out on my back, his mouth on mine. He kisses me hard, harder than earlier, and his tongue slides into my mouth. I snake my hands around his back. His skin is burning hot and moist and dammit, I hate that he's still dressed. I want to explore more of him.

As if reading my mind, he stands, and kicks his pants off. He goes still for a moment, gifting me a view of his gorgeous, cut body.

"Your turn," he murmurs.

I blink up at him, my brain on hiatus until he gives me a sexy grin. "Right," I say, and reach for the hem of the house dress. I suddenly realize I'm about to get naked and I stop.

"Sawyer?" he asks, his breathing rough and erratic. He swallows and runs his hand over his face. "Change of heart?" He inches back, and I appreciate the gesture, and the look of concern in his eyes. Underneath that rock hard exterior, he's a nice guy, maybe even a softie, and I have zero doubts that I chose the right guy for my first time, because everything in his body language tells me that if I want to stop, he's going to stop despite the raging erection between his legs.

Do you want to stop, Sawyer?

My sex throbs, telling me in no uncertain terms what it wants, and it brings a small grin to my face. Chase's gaze moves over my face, and he smiles too, understanding that I want him...tonight. No regrets.

Answering without words, I tug the dress up and over my head, and my entire body quivers at his hungry response. His hand goes to his cheek and he scrubs his face as his gaze leisurely rakes over the length of me, taking his time to examine every inch, and from the darkening of his eyes, it's easy to tell he likes what he sees.

I reach for my panties, and he shakes his head to stop me. I angle my head. He doesn't want me to take them off? How are we supposed to fool around, or whatever one calls this? I'm about to question him, but stop when I spot the mischief dancing in his eyes.

His grin is slow and playful and my body heats up, loving everything about this. "You've talked so much about your panties that I'm going to need an extra moment to check them out." Heat flushes through me as he climbs on the bed.

Moving me like I weigh no more than a rag doll, he centers me on the mattress, pushes my thighs apart and groans as he fingers the very boring, very plain piece of cotton.

Oh God, oh God, oh God. Why didn't I have the foresight to wear something sexy? Honestly, even if I knew I was going to be stranded and rescued by the hottest guy on the planet, I still would have worn boring white panties. That's all I own. But I'm not sure he sees boring white when he looks me over. He's studying my underwear like they're the hottest piece of cotton on the face of the earth. Just how long has it been since he's been with a girl anyway? That has to be why he seems so mesmerized, right?

One thick warm finger slides under the waist band, and the heat from his finger sizzles my flesh as he tugs the cotton from hip to hip. He drags my panties down an inch, exposing the top of my pubic bone. I go up on my elbows, my heart racing. At least I trimmed down there, with the expectation that I'd be spending a week in my bathing suit.

"Do you want to show me how you touch yourself?"

I actually want him to touch me, but since he showed me what he does, it's only fair that I show him what I do. He seems super stoked by the idea. I slide my hand down my stomach, and he pulls on the band of my panties to grant me access. Why is that so damn hot? His eyes blaze with heat as I reach down and stroke my soaking wet clit. I'm not sure I've ever been so wet or so excited. I had no idea how much I'd love doing this in front of someone. I must say, I'm not sure I could do it in front of just any guy. Chase is easy to be around, and I don't feel judged. I don't feel like the chubby girl that no guy wanted to kiss, or the coach's daughter that guys dared one another to bag.

"Feel good, Sawyer?"

"Yes," I manage to get out.

"Do you come when you touch yourself?"

I shut my eyes and concentrate on the sensations. "I think so."

There's warmth and sincerity in his eyes as they meet mine. "You're not sure?" he asks.

My lids jerk open. "It always feels good."

He tugs at my panties until my sex is completely exposed and he briefly closes his eyes and takes a breath. My finger works my clit, and he takes my hand and puts it on my stomach. A keening cry catches in my throat as he puts his big, callused thumb on my nub and applies pressure as he rubs it in a circle.

"Holy," I say.

"Now look who's praying," he teases.

"That feels way better than when I do it."

His other hand goes to my nether lips and he spreads them, taking his time to examine me. "So pretty, and so wet." His head lifts, his gaze back on mine. "No guy has ever put his tongue here?" He runs his fingers up and down my sex, as he continues to press his thumb against my clit, and I swear to God, it's all so much I can't think straight, and really, I don't care to.

"No, never."

He pulls back, his hands no longer on my body. Oh no, he's changed his mind. He doesn't want to be my first. I reach for him, my words catching in my throat as he pushes my legs together and slides my panties down my legs and off my feet. The next thing I know, he's on his stomach with my knees bent, his hands under my ass. He lifts my body to his mouth, and that first sweet lick of his hot tongue catapults me into outer space where nothing exists but pleasure.

Why haven't I been doing this during all my college years?

Oh, I remember now. Guys don't pay me attention. But that thought is for another day, when Chase isn't making up for a lifetime of being overlooked—with his tongue.

Oh wait, what was that?

7

CHASE

My God, she's the sweetest thing I've ever tasted. I lap at her, unable to get enough. Her body quivers as I run my tongue over her, but the second I slide a finger into her tight pussy, she goes completely still. I glance up, my thumb still on her clit, my finger still in her tight core.

"Sawyer, you with me?" I ask, her eyes big, her mouth gaping open. "Sawyer?"

"That...that feels incredible," she says as she grips the bedding and holds on tight. I chuckle as I begin to stroke the hot bundle of nerves inside her body, wanting to make this good for her. I was shocked by her questions at first—inexperienced yes, but shy she isn't—and I wasn't going to answer until I saw real curiosity. I don't know how a girl as sweet and as beautiful as Sawyer has gone this long without being touched. One part of me is sad that she's missed out on pleasure, the other side is glad that she chose me as her first.

I work my tongue over her and keep glancing up to check in on her. Her eyes are dazed, as she goes to a faraway place where reality no longer exists. She's so different from the girls I know in Boston, and I really like her.

I move against the bed, my cock so hard I could shoot off just from the taste of her alone. Christ, it was all I could do to hang on, and not think about math when she put her mouth on me. I had to pull her off, before I came in her throat. While I would have liked that, I'm not sure she's ready for that, and she probably would have hated it. I don't want this experience to leave a bad taste in her mouth, so to speak.

I work my finger inside her. It's a good thing we're not fucking. She's so tiny and tight I might destroy her, and in no way would I want to hurt her. "Talk to me, Sawyer. Tell me what you like."

"I like...I like your finger in me. I like what you're doing to my clit." She tosses her head from side to side, and I take my finger from her clit. "No," she whimpers in protest.

"How about this?" I put my mouth on her clit and slide my hand up to play with her nipple.

"Oh yes, I like that." I angle my head in time to see her take her other breast into her hand. She squeezes her nipple, and I do the same thing to her other breast. Her whimper of delight fills the room and I dive deeper into her pussy, rocking against the bed as I eat at her. The headboard bangs against the wall, and we both still. A second later, a chuckle rumbles out of her throat and I laugh too.

"Now it's our turn to keep them up," she says playfully.

"Oh, I'm up, Sawyer. I'm totally up." My fucking cock is aching, urging me to slide inside her. I work to satisfy my throbbing dick by rubbing against the bed, but it wants more.

"Your cock...is it still uncomfortable?"

"I'm okay," I answer, and swirl my tongue around her clit until she's lost in pleasure again, thinking only of herself—for now.

"Chase, I'm on fire," she says, as small quakes begin in her core and ripple down my finger. She's close, she's so fucking close to her first orgasm. If she wasn't sure if she'd ever had one, chances are she didn't. She'd remember this kind of pleasure.

I pinch her nipple a little harder and slide my tongue over her clit as my finger massages her aroused nerve endings.

She gasps. "I can't...it's too much." I keep working her, her entire body shaking as her orgasm builds. She sucks in a breath, and I eat at her like a man starved. "Chase," she cries out, loud enough that I'm sure the guests on both sides of our room can hear us through the paper-thin walls.

Her body squeezes tight around my finger, and a keening cry curls around me as she lets go and comes all over my face and hand. I stay between her legs, finger fucking her as slowly as she rides out the waves. I hear her swallow against a dry throat, and I pull my finger out and lightly pet her sweet pussy to ease any sting left behind.

I go up on my knees, my hands on her thighs as her body remains wide open for me, and my gaze settles on her gorgeous tits.

"Chase, that was..." She shakes her head. "That was an orgasm." Her lips curl, her eyes full of sated warmth. "I can't believe it."

"No?"

"It felt good when I touched myself, but I never had that kind of explosion before."

I laugh quietly, hardly able to believe she's telling me such personal, intimate things. "You're going to have to teach me how to do that so I can do that to myself every single day."

My heart pounds against my ribs at her sweet innocence. "How about this..." I begin, as she stares at me, eager to hear more. "I'll do it for you."

Her nose crinkles. "But you won't always be around."

"True, but I mean for as long as we're stranded here." I lightly run my finger over her wet sex. "I'll do this for you." She tugs on her bottom lip with her teeth. Shit, did I push for too much, cross a line? "Unless you don't want me to."

"Oh, I do," she says, her eyes wide. "I just want to do it for you too."

Jesus, who is this woman?

I grip my cock, and start stroking it. Her gaze drops, captivated by what I'm doing. She likes watching, and I like her watching me. "I'm so close, Sawyer, if you put one little finger on me, I'm going to lose it, and right now, I want to come all over your gorgeous tits." Her chest expands as she sucks in air, and I groan. "Squeeze them for me, babe." As I jerk off, I'm a little shocked at myself. I'm saying things to Sawyer that I've never said to any other girl.

She does as I ask. "Tomorrow though? I get to do things to your cock?"

"Christ, girl. Yes."

"You'll let me suck you."

"Uh huh."

"Do you think I would like or hate it if you came in my mouth?"

Christ, I can't believe the questions that come out of her mouth. I stroke my dick faster, pleasure gripping every nerve in my body as she talks dirty to me, and the fact that she doesn't even realize she's talking dirty makes it that much hotter.

"Some...uh... do, some..." I grunt with pleasure. "...don't." I work to form a sentence as my vocabulary fails me.

"I supposed I should try it though, right? To figure out if I'm going to like it." She nods, like she's already made up her mind. "I think I will."

"Fuck me," I groan, as my body lets go and I shoot my cum all over her lush tits. She stares in pure fascination, and if I'm not mistaken, pride. She likes what she does to me. Hell, I like what she does to me too.

I throw my head back as I keep spurting and spurting and just when I think I'm done, I spurt a little bit more. I swear I've never come like that in my entire life. Her legs squeeze around me as my come drips over her nipples.

"It's hot," she says, and I shake my head. Her innocence is going to be the death of me.

"You're hot," I say and fall over her, putting my hands on her sides to keep from squishing her. I kiss her, deeply, and our tongues leisurely tangle and play. With sweat dampening our bodies, and the air in the room cooling us even more, I inch back. "I'd suggest a shower, but I don't think that's too safe in the dark and the water is probably cold now anyway."

"Agreed." She makes a move to get up, but I lightly press down on her.

"You wait here. I'll get a warm cloth to clean you up."

She settles back on the bed, and I scoop up the flashlight. I make a fast trip to the bathroom to wash myself off, and fill a glass with water. I take a sip, put a cloth under the water and make my way back to Sawyer. I shine my light on her to find her laying there, with a smile on her face.

I hope the roads never get plowed.

That thought takes me by surprise. I need to get to the city, to the academy to check it out and go a few rounds with the team to see if it's for me. While I like being here with Sawyer, it will eventually come to an end, and I have a future to think about. I should be praying the roads get plowed—tonight.

I grab a few tissues from the box on the nightstand and wipe my cum from her body. She shivers. "You okay?"

Her shoulders tighten, a slight chatter to her teeth when she says, "It's getting cold in here."

"Let me clean you up and I'll warm you." I toss the tissues away, and use the cloth on her body, washing her stomach, breasts, and sex.

She giggles. "That's not supposed to be turning me on, right?"

"I think you need sleep."

She tries to stifle a yawn. "I think I do, too. It's been a long hard day." She chuckles again. "And a long hard night."

I just shake my head at her joke, and once she's clean I hand her the glass of water and she takes a big drink. "Thanks, I was so dry."

I slide in beside her, and she starts to fix the pillows between us again. What the hell? After I've had my mouth and hands all over her and vice versa, she wants to separate us.

"Uh, Sawyer."

I shine the light on her, to see her face. She blinks up at me, innocence all over her. "Yes?"

"Do you think we still need the pillows?" She bites her lip, trying to hide a smile. "Oh I get it. You're messing with me."

I pick a pillow up and lightly hit her with it.

She laughs and grabs it from me. "You just make it too easy, Chase."

"Are you saying I'm gullible or something?"

I pull her to me and she settles against my shoulder. I cover us with the blankets and hold her tight, giving her my warmth. She snuggles in tighter, and I smooth a hand over her hair as it tickles my face.

She exhales a contented sigh. "No, I'm saying you're easy."

"Yeah, I guess I am. I swore to myself I wouldn't touch you, and all you had to do was talk dirty to me," I tease.

"Were you thinking about math, or the blizzard?"

"Not even close. Were you?" I ask.

"No."

"Whew."

She laughs quietly, and we both fall quiet, lost in our own thoughts. As the wind blows, and the snow-laden trees brush against the building, my body calms in a way it hasn't calmed in a very long time and I can't help but want to know more about her.

"Do you live in Halifax?" I ask. I've just had oral sex with a girl I like very much but know little about. It's been a long time since I had a hook-up and even longer since I've wanted to know more about a girl.

"I do." She runs her finger along my stomach, and I shiver as she tickles me. "Born and raised."

I take her finger and bring it to my mouth, kissing it gently. "You like it there?"

She nods and her hair tickles me again. "It's a great place from April to November." She glances up at me and crinkles her nose. "Then...snow. I hate snow."

"If you don't like snow, why do you stay there?"

"There's a great theater program. Best in the country, actually. After that, maybe I'll move to Florida where it's warm."

"You're in theater?" I don't know why that surprises me so much.

"Yeah, forget I said that. It's boring." She waves her hand like she doesn't want to discuss it. "I never should have said anything."

"Yes, you should have. If it's important to you, I want to know Oh wait, are you saying that because you were acting with me, pretending to have an orgasm?" I tease, knowing very well she wasn't. The way her body let go can't be faked, and I take pride in knowing that.

She whacks my chest. "No, of course not."

"I think that's really cool, Sawyer."

She lifts her head, rests her palms on my chest and puts her chin on them. "Really?"

"I don't know anyone in theater. I could never do it."

"Why not?"

I toy with her hair, putting it behind her ear and messing it up again as I debate on how much to tell her. I like this honesty between us, and I could ruin it with one simple word. Hockey. Like I said before, people instantly change when they know my dad was in the NHL, and that I'm on my way there myself. I like Sawyer just the way she is. Open, easy, no judgement. I don't want to jeopardize any of that.

"I wouldn't be any good at it. I don't like being the center of attention."

"You liked being the center of attention tonight," she teases as she tilts her head coyly.

"That's different. All those people watching you..." I feign a shiver. "I prefer one on one." On the rink, numerous people watch and cheer. I somehow tune them out and can focus on the game. In theater, you play to the audience. I hate everything about that.

"I love acting. On the stage, I can be anyone I want to be."

"Why would you want to be anyone else but yourself?"

She smiles and puts her head back down and I get the sense she has more to say on the subject but doesn't want to. I get it. There are things I could tell her but don't want to either.

"Have you been in any big productions?"

She nods, but doesn't say any more, and I leave it at that. I turn the flashlight off and close my eyes. While I'm tired and usually sleep after sex, tonight I find myself wide awake. Which totally sucks because for the first time in a long time, I'm looking forward to tomorrow—no responsibilities, no game, just Sawyer and me trapped in this motel with nothing to do but...

Bang. Bang. Bang.

Her body vibrates as she chuckles against me. "They're at it again."

As I listen, my dick thickens, and with her leg thrown over me, there's no way I can hide it. Truthfully, it's not the neighbors fucking that is turning me on. No, it's just having Sawyer here with me, my worries temporarily on hold, as the storm keeps us hostage.

"It's going to be a long, hard night," I say with a sigh.

Her body moves and her fingers curl around my thickening dick. "Speaking of hard..."

"Jesus, Sawyer."

"Looks like you have an *erection*."

I laugh and shake my head. Great, now every time I hear the word erection, I'm going to salivate like Pavlov's dogs. Here I thought Sawyer was sweet and innocent, but now, as I roll her beneath me, I'm beginning to suspect she loves torturing me.

I smooth her hair back and take in her playful grin. "If you know what's good for you, Sawyer, you'd stop saying that."

"Erection."

8

SAWYER

Voices pull me awake and I open one eye slowly. Where the hell am I? As memories of last night come flooding back, I quickly turn my head, my gaze settling on Chase sleeping soundly beside me and looking so adorable and innocent. I shift, and an ache flares through my body as muscles that I didn't know existed groan in protest. I smile, unable to help myself. Last night was unlike any other I'd ever experienced and while I don't know what other people do or say in bed, I'm pretty sure things were perfect between us. I've never done a morning after, so I don't know if things will be awkward or not. I guess we'll soon find out.

I slowly push the blankets aside, not wanting to wake Chase, and tug on his sweater, which hangs just below my ass. There's a calmness to this frosty morning, a silence that falls over me as I move quietly. The cold seeps into my bones as I tip-toe to the window and inch the curtains open to peek out. I wince as the sun glints off the high snowbanks, nearly blinding me. Trees sway in the distance, snow weighing down their branches, and from the looks of things, we might be stranded in this motel until spring. I hate winter, but even I have to admit, the view before me is gorgeous.

"Don't move."

"What?" I angle my head to find Chase climbing from the bed, and my gaze drops to take in his naked body.

"Don't move," he says again and comes up behind me. His big arms wrap around my body, warming me, and I lean into him to soak in his heat. I guess things aren't going to be awkward at all. He moves my hair to the side, and lightly presses his lips to my neck and a fine shiver goes through me.

"Cold?"

"Yes, but that's not why I'm shivering."

He laughs, his warm breath falling over my flesh. "I'm going to check on the generator today, and you need clothes."

"I can't go out there in that house dress again. Not in the light of day," I say.

"I have sweats you can wear."

"You're only just telling me this now? You mean I didn't have to wear that ridiculous dress yesterday, and make a spectacle of myself?"

He spins me, his dark eyes moving over my face. "I liked the dress on you."

"Liar," I snort and smack him. "You're going to pay for that."

He grins. "Want to head down to the lobby and see what's happening with the roads and get something to eat?"

I finger comb my hair. I can't even imagine what it must look like this morning, but I'm not sure Chase cares. I reach out and smooth his hair down. How is a guy who looks like him still single? I don't know, but I plan to take advantage of him until we get out of here.

He steps away, grabs me a big pair of sweatpants and a T-shirt and tosses them my way. He makes a quick trip to the bathroom, and when he comes out, his hair combed, and he's dressed in jeans and a sweater. I take a moment to admire him. He snatches up his phone.

"Still no service," he says. "Mine's about to die anyway."

"It could be days before we have power. I still have lots of battery, but no service." I step into the small bathroom and turn on the taps. "At least we have running water. It might be cold, but it's better than nothing." The thoughts of showering in cold water sends chills through me. "I really hope you get the generator going." I like that he's mechanically inclined and good with his hands. My dad is a handyman like that, too. He'd probably really like Chase. I shake my head. What the hell am I saying? The two are never going to meet.

I brush my teeth and wash my body in cold water, and I'm freezing by the time I climb into his sweats. I step from the bathroom and spread my arms to showcase his baggy clothes.

He smiles. "My sweats look good on you." He steps up to me and runs the backs of his knuckles over my cheek. "I look good on you."

I go up on my toes, and kiss him, tasting minty toothpaste on his tongue. "Yeah, you do," I say. My sex tingles as I relive the things Chase did to me last night. Tonight, I'm hoping for that, and much more.

I grab the key from the desk and we step into the hall. As we make our way to the main lobby, voices reach our ears. I spot Danielle and Trev warming by the fire. Did they hear us last night? I should probably be embarrassed by that, but why bother? They started it.

The elderly couple Chase gave his room to, are sitting on the sofa, and Betsy is in a comfy chair beside them. She smiles when she sees us. "Chase, Sawyer, good morning. How did you sleep?"

"Great," I say, even though we'd gotten so little of it, and Chase agrees.

"Any news on the roads?" Chase asks as he walks to the big front window and looks out. I'm sure he must be anxious to get to the city and start his vacation. I should be anxious too. It's strange that I'm not. But I'm having fun passing the time away.

"Afraid not," Betsy says. "I heard from Malcolm and it's going to take some time for the machinery to get up the mountain. It's one of the biggest snowfalls Nova Scotia has seen in decades. He says it's something like fifty centimeters so far, and up here on the mountain, you can double that. They are just getting to the Trans-Canada and he doesn't expect they'll be finished there before nightfall. But we have plenty of food, and water, and heat from the fire."

Chase glances at me. "One hundred centimeters?"

I do the math, not that math is my thing. "Around forty inches, give or take."

"Jesus." He shakes his head, surprised.

The last time we had this much snow the province was shut down for days. We were very lucky we got to this motel when we did. I'm lucky Chase happened to drive by when he did. I shiver to think what could have happened if I had blacked out in the car, or tried to walk here in the dark.

"Do you mind if I take a look at the generator?" he asks Betsy.

"Not at all. Come on, it's in the storage shed right out back." She tightens a knitted shawl around her shoulders. "You might want to put more on than that. You'll have to go outside."

"I'll help," Trev says and jumps up.

As the two guys head back to their rooms to grab their coats, I take Trev's place on the brick platform in front of the roaring fire. I twist to the side and hold my hands out. The warmth washes over me as I fold up the sleeves on the sweater up.

Danielle leans into me, her words hushed, for my ears only. She grins almost coyly, and says, "I hope we didn't keep you guys up last night."

"No, not at all," I lie, knowing we probably kept them up too. "I'm so sorry that you guys got stuck here for your honeymoon. Where were you going?"

"Jamaica. We're trying to make the best of it here, though."

"I was on my way to Florida."

"Bummer." She glances up as a middle-aged couple come down the stairs, Chase and Trev behind them. "Chase is cute."

I grin. "Yeah, I think so too."

"How long have you two been together?"

"We kind of just met," I admit, and wrinkle my nose, slightly embarrassed. "He gave his room up last night, so he bunked with me."

Her eyes go wide and she nudges me. "Get it, gurl."

I laugh at that, any embarrassment I felt gone. I like her, a lot. More people come to the main lobby, filling it up. At least there's room for everyone. I look at Danielle and try to figure out how I can be useful while Chase and Trev head down the hall with Betsy. "Should we go see what we can make for breakfast for everyone?"

"You bet." She pushes to her feet and I follow her up. We make our way down the corridor leading to the café, and I note that this morning she's dressed in the same jeans and a sweater as last night.

"I take it you didn't pack for winter."

"I packed for the beach," she says.

"Same. That's why I'm in Chase's clothes. My suitcase is still in my car. Not that it will do me much good, but it does have my makeup and toiletries that could be useful."

We step into the kitchen and Danielle goes straight for the stove. "It's gas," she announces with a happy squeal. "We can cook." I honestly don't know the first thing about gas stoves. I step up to it and touch the dials. "Um... She laughs. "Don't worry. I know how to use it."

"Are you a chef?" I ask.

"Sous chef, at Azure."

My jaw drops open. "No way. I love that place." I shake my head. "Small world and how lucky that we got stranded with a chef."

She turns the stove on, and gets a flame going. "If we don't get power, we can put the food into boxes and put it outside. It'll stay cold."

"Smart idea." I step up to the fridge. I'm about to open it, but go still when the lights overhead flicker. I hold my breath, praying for them to come on, but they shut off. "Darn." I grab eggs, and bacon and some tomatoes and vegetables. "Omelet up," I announce. The lights flicker again. And once again, they go off. I kind of liked our night in the dark, but it would be nice to have electricity again...and coffee. I gaze longingly at the coffee pots.

"Why don't you check with the guests to make sure there are no allergies, and I'll cook up breakfast for everyone."

"On it," I say and salute her as I make my way back, and run into Betsy as she comes through a door in the hallway, a cold breeze following her in. "How are they making out? I saw the lights flicker."

She frowns and wrings her gnarled fingers together before tightening her shawl over her shoulders. "They're fiddling." She makes a tsking sound. "Billy could never keep that thing running." Once again, I want to ask about Billy, but since he hasn't surfaced yet, I suspect he's no longer with us, or maybe he just stays in his room.

Don't think about Bates motel, Sawyer!

I seriously watch to many horror movies. "Danielle is a sous chef and knows how to work the stove and she's going to cook breakfast for us all." Just then the door in the hallway opens again, and it's weird how my entire body jumps to attention, every nerve on hyperdrive as Chase fills the hallway. What is it that's so appealing about a man who is big and strong and good with his hands anyway?

"Hey." I smile, feeling like a silly schoolgirl with a crush.

"Good news and bad news," he says, Trev moving in beside him, while the cold radiates off them.

I fold my arms across my chest as a cool breeze chills me to my bones. "Let's go with the good first." Chase grins at me, and I get it, I'm being a glass half full girl this morning, but after last night, I'm in a good mood, despite being snowed in and missing my girl's trip.

"We got the generator going, but the gas is old," Chase explains.

"Is there a gas station nearby?" Trev asks as he kicks snow off his boots.

"Yeah, but how can we get there?" I remember passing a gas station last night. The lights were still on, and they probably have a generator for backup. If anyone was there last night, they're likely stuck. "We can't walk anywhere, and our cars won't go two feet."

"Does that snowmobile work?" Chase asks Betsy. "I saw it under the back deck."

"Billy hasn't used that in years," she says, and looks off into the distance like she's remembering good times from the past.

"If the gas station isn't too far, I could use the old generator gas in the snowmobile. It probably has enough to get there, and there's a sled attachment that I can use to bring jerry cans back here."

"Is there enough gas to get you there and back?" I ask. He shakes his head, unsure. "What if the gas station isn't open?"

"I think it's a chance I'll have to take. These people need warmth, especially the older ones, and we can keep the generator going for a few hours at a time to heat water."

I think it's sweet that he cares about the others. "I'll go with you."

Chase angles his head, and frowns. "I'm not sure that's a great idea."

I put my hands on my hips. "Do you know where this gas station is?" I ask.

"No, but I can find it. Just give me directions."

"I know this area better than you. You're not freezing to death on my watch."

"You don't even have a hat or mitts," he points out. I eye him because yeah, he doesn't either.

"Oh, darlings..." Betsy begins, and points up at the ceiling. "There are boxes and boxes of clothing in the attic. Left here by guests over the years. You just help yourself to whatever you need."

"Perfect," I say and lift my chin an inch. I realize Chase is considering my best interests and there's no point in us both freezing to death, but I grew up in Nova Scotia. There isn't much I can't handle.

"Are you sure, Sawyer?" Chase asks, his brow arched. "If we get stuck, there's no point in the two of us trekking back here in the snow."

"You think I'm going to slow you down?"

"No," he says. "I'll probably slow you down."

I grin, liking his confidence in me, but he's just kidding. He's built and fit, and could probably piggyback me for ten miles and not even get winded.

I hold my arm up and showcase my Fitbit. "I need the steps. Besides, two heads are better than one, and what if one of us needs body warmth for survival?"

He just laughs. "I don't know about your logic."

"I can help," Trev says, finally get a chance to break into the conversation.

"Do you know the way?" I ask.

He scrunches up his face. "Not really."

"Okay, I'm going then."

"You're really sure?" Chase asks.

"Positive. Danielle is making breakfast." I jerk my thumb toward the main lobby. "I'm checking in with guests on allergies. After we eat, we can go get gas." Trev heads toward the kitchen and Betsy makes her way to the lobby. I'm about to follow her when Chase captures my arm and pulls me to him.

"It's going to be a rough ride on that old snowmobile. You sure you want to come?"

I hold my finger out and circle my face. "Does anything about me say I'm afraid of hard?"

He grins, and I know, just like I am, he's thinking about last night. He makes a fist and nudges my chin. "Canadian girls. So tough." Catching me by surprise, he dips his head, and presses his cold lips to mine. I grip the front of his jacket, and kiss him back. A girl could get used to this kind of attention. But this is just a weekend fling, two people passing the time away in a snowstorm. While I'd prefer it on the beach, this isn't bad at all.

Footsteps reach my ears and I pull back, and glance to my left to see all the guests headed our way. "Breakfast," I say, and I turn to do a quick tally. There looks to be about fourteen of us here altogether.

I lead them all into the café, and we all do a round of introductions and I find out about allergies before I head back to the back kitchen to help Danielle. I push the door open to find her and Trev kissing and I stand there and smile. They're so cute together. Chase follows me in, and they break apart.

"Sorry," Danielle says, blushing.

I just laugh it off and ask what I can do to help. She puts Chase and me on juice duty, and after he shrugs out of his winter jacket, we fill the pitchers and bring them out to the guests. Many of them are elderly, and I'm glad they made it to the motel and aren't stuck on the highway, cold, hungry and frightened. Then again, they'd be plowed out quicker there than here.

As Chase fills the glasses, an elderly man—I think I heard someone call him Frank—says, "Do I know you?"

"Nope, just visiting. I'm not from around these parts," Chase tells him and I turn to him, noting the way he's suddenly uncomfortable. He averts his gaze and goes on to the next table. Strange. I quickly forget about it as one of the elderly lady glances at me, and says, "I hope we get out of here soon. This place gives me the creeps. Heard nothing but banging all night."

The pitcher of juice nearly falls from my hand, and I quickly set it on the table. "Old places creak," I tell her.

"Well, I don't like it."

"Florence," the man across from her says, and I assume it's her husband. "I don't know what you think you heard. You snored all night."

She waves the end of her silk scarf at him. "You're the one who snored, not me."

I dart back to the kitchen as they fight it out, and my stomach grumbles as delicious smells reach my nostrils. "We're stranded with a chef," I tell Chase as he steps up beside me.

"Yeah, Trev told me. He also told me he's a mechanic, which was very helpful in fixing the generator."

"What do you do, Chase?" Danielle asks as Trev delivers plates of food,

"Student. Trev mentioned he's originally from Alberta." I eye Chase, noticing the way he turned the conversation away from himself. He did say he didn't like being the center of attention.

"That's right." A warmth moves into Danielle's eyes. "He grew up on a farm."

"That's cool."

Chase has a longing look in his eyes. Does he want to be a farmer or something?

"You and Trev sound like you hit it off," I say.

"Yeah, we did actually."

Danielle plates up a bunch of omelets, as Trev comes back, and as he says something to his wife, I say to Chase, "I like Danielle too. She works at one of my favorite restaurants."

"Order up," Danielle says.

Chase and I scoop up the plates and start delivering them. Once everyone is fed, Danielle cooks for the four of us, and we all grab a table in the café. I just met all three people I'm sitting with, yet I'm so comfortable with them, and of course one of them has seen me naked.

"I am dying for a hot shower," Danielle says as she takes a sip of her juice. She stares at the cup. "And I wish this was coffee."

"Me too," I say. "With any luck, we'll get the generator going, and we can get heat, water and something hot to drink."

"We're going to have to conserve electricity and water," Trev says. "The gas will only go so far, which means..." he lets his words fall off and I stare at him, waiting for him to finish. When he doesn't, I turn to Chase, and he's grinning.

"We'll have to conserve, too," he tells me. I narrow my eyes, still not getting it.

"Okay."

"The best way to conserve water is by showering together," he explains, a devilish grin on his face, that sends excitement racing through me.

I bite my lip. "Wow, who knew roughing it would be so hard." Chase's leg brushes mine, and my pulse jumps.

"Yeah, real hard," Chase agrees, his eyes telegraphing a private message that I should prepare for things to get really hard later.

I can't wait.

9

CHASE

"Here, this toque is thick and perfect," Sawyer says, and pulls a hat from one of the many boxes in the attic and tosses it my way.

"Toque," I snicker as I shake the dust from the wool and put it on my head. "If I move here, do you think I'll start talking like you?" Shit, why would I bring up moving here? I honestly have no idea if I'll be transferring here next semester or not. I told her I was here to visit a friend, and I should leave it at that. We're having fun, and I'm the hook-up she was supposed to find in Florida. Talking about moving here might scare her off, or have her thinking I'm looking for more after our time here ends. Neither one of us are looking for that.

She puts one hand on her hip, and glares at me. I have no idea what's going through her mind, and suspect she's about to give me an earful, but then something falls from the ceiling, and she jumps up and starts dancing around, whacking at her hair and clothes.

"What is it? Is it a spider? Ohmigod, Chase, get it off me."

I jump to my feet, and try to look her over as she hops around, nearly tripping over the numerous boxes, and a few sleds propped up nearby. "I think it's just dust." I tug what looks to be a dried-up spider's web from her hair. I don't want to tell her what it is, she's freaking out enough as it is. "It's gone," I say and shake it off my hand. I put my hands on her shoulders to still her.

She crouches and looks overhead, a shiver going through her. "God knows what's living up here."

I look at the exposed beams overhead as I rub my hands up and down her arms to create heat with friction. "I'm not sure much can survive in these freezing temperatures."

Her focus turns to me. "Cockroaches survived the ice age, Chase."

"You don't know that."

"I do know that." She drops down, grabs another hat from the box, inspects it thoroughly, and shakes it before she puts it on her head. "What's wrong with the way I talk?"

Ah, so that's what she was going to say to me. "Nothing, eh?"

She laughs. "That's not how you use eh."

I tear into a box and just grin at her. "Look at all these skates."

She stares at the skates, but her brows knit together. "Wait, did you say something about moving here? I thought you said you were just visiting a friend."

Shit. "My buddy Brandon is here in Halifax." I shrug like it's nothing. I'm enjoying our time together, with her getting to know the real me. Granted I didn't tell her who or what I really am, or that I was studying business in Boston, or that if

I transferred, I'd want to change disciplines. My parents don't believe animal science is a great career choice for after hockey, whether I make the NHL, or not. But it's what really interests me, and I just want to carve my own path. "He's trying to talk me into transferring."

"Oh."

She goes quiet, and I panic and say, "I like the programs at the academy."

She nods, like she can understand that. "Is that why he's here? For the programs?"

I nod, It's not a lie. I'm just omitting the other reason he's at Scotia Academy. She opens her mouth, like she's going to ask more questions, and I pull a big wool sweater from the box. "Here, this will keep you warm, especially if we have to walk back." She eyes me for another second before her gaze strays to the sweater. A smile touches her mouth. "What?" I ask.

"I haven't seen a lopi in years," she says quietly, almost dreamily.

"Lopi, is that a Canadian thing?"

She snatches it from me, and shakes it out. "Lopi is a type of yarn. You've never heard of it?"

"Nope."

"My grandmother used to knit these for me when I was a kid. I had dozens of them."

Her lids fall slightly, a small smile touching her mouth as she holds the sweater. "You miss her, huh?"

"I do." She stands and tugs on the heavy wool sweater.

"Fits you perfectly."

She steps up to the old mirror propped up in the corner and examines herself. "My mom had one just like this."

"Maybe it's hers. Maybe she left it here years ago."

"Yeah, maybe." Her mood changes quickly, and I stiffen as sadness comes over her. Was it something I said? She'd mentioned her mother before, when she was talking about clean underwear. I assumed it was a safe topic, but maybe it's not. Maybe they had a fight, or something worse...

She goes quiet as she roots through the boxes and finds some wool socks and mitts for both of us. I shut my mouth, not wanting to upset her any more than I have. I find a box full of board games and cards, and she pulls a sequined dress from the box she's rooting through, and her mood shifts again. "Look at this. It's perfect."

"For what? The eighties?"

She laughs. "Last year, I worked at a dinner theater and we wore dresses like this."

"Maybe you could put it on tonight and dance and sing as we eat dinner." Her eyes light up. "Wait, I was only kidding."

She shrugs. "Could be fun. Something to pass the time. Do it with me?"

"I don't think that dress will fit me, but I'm sure you'll be great." I grin as I take in her smile, happy to see her sparkling again. "I admire anyone who can get on a stage and do what you do, Sawyer. Your parents must be so proud." Shit, didn't mean to bring up her parents. Her smile disappears from her face at the mention of her mother.

She sighs and her fingers curl in the dress as her hands fall to her lap. "Dad wants me to be a professional curler."

"Really?"

"Yup."

"It's not for you?"

"I like it, but don't want to go professional. I enjoy theater."

"Then you should do theatre."

She laughs. "Can you tell that to my father?" She rolls the dress up and sets it aside. "When we get back from the service station, I want to go through more boxes."

"We can do that." I pull my phone from my pocket and check the time. "But we should get going. We don't want to get stuck out there in the dark."

"Right." She jumps up and bundles up all the clothes. I go down the rickety stairs first and hold my hand out to catch her if she falls on her way down. I close the attic, and we make our way to the main lobby to get dressed and ready to go out in the cold. The room is empty except for Betsy, who is reading in her big comfy chair near the logs burning in the fire.

"You two be careful out there, and you should take some snacks just in case. Let me grab you both some granola bars and juice packs."

"She's right," I agree. We bundle up, and Sawyer wobbles in all the layers as she walks over to Betsy, who is back with an armload of refreshments. She fills our pockets and we head outdoors. I wince as a cold gust of wind washes over me, and turn to check on Sawyer, worried she's going to blow away.

I take her hand in mine before she's blown over the mountain. She's so tiny I expect her to take flight any second. I tug her along, but she keeps pace, fighting the wind as I snatch up the old gas can from the shed, and duck under the deck, to pull back the tarp on the snowmobile. After I fill the tank and get it going, I hook up the sled to the back of it and jump on. Sawyer climbs on behind me, and hugs me tight with her arms and legs.

I take off and the snowmobile sputters at first, but then I get it out into the open snow and it's pretty smooth sailing. From behind me, Sawyer yells out directions, and I cut through the forest on the winding trails until we're on the snow-covered road. We follow the road and I keep a close eye on the gas gauge. We travel for a good five miles, and I'm pretty much on fumes when I see the gas station sign up ahead. I tap Sawyer's knee, thrilled that we made it, and she hugs me tighter. I ease into the gas station and park the snowmobile at the frosty pumps.

"It looks empty," Sawyer says, as I climb off the machine, and hold my hand out to help her. I stand there and consider our next move when I hear a dog bark from inside.

"Shit, I hope he's not alone in there." I trek through the deep snow, Sawyer behind me walking in my tracks, as we walk up to the glass door, and I put my hand over my eyes to see in. A dog jumps up, and Sawyer and I step backward as it scares the shit out of us.

"Easy. Buster," I hear from inside.

"Someone is in there," I say.

"Thank God."

The lock clicks and the door opens. "Get in here, you two and warm up," a tall thin man who looks to be around forty says and fixes his ball cap as he ushers us in. His dog, a gorgeous German Shepard, barks once at us, and I take my mitts off.

"Hey Buster," I say. Buster's ears perk, and he sniffs my hand. I crouch down, and give him a rub.

"He likes you." The man nods and smiles, like he's pleased by that. "He doesn't like too many people."

"I like animals." Buster sticks his tongue out and licks me, showing me just how much he likes me in return. I laugh and wipe my face and note the way Sawyer stands back a bit. I can't blame her. Buster is a scary looking dude.

"You two stuck out in this weather," the guy asks.

I stand, and jerk my thumb out. "We're at the motel. No power. We're hoping to fill up on fuel to get the generator going."

"Pumps are shut down but I can turn them on. Heard the Trans-Canada is a mess." He mumbles something about government building a highway in the highest elevation area, and I'm sure he used the word idiots.

"Are you okay here?" Sawyer asks. "Do you need anything?"

"Got everything we need." I glance around the small grocery store, and don't miss the way Sawyer is eyeing the coffee pot.

"Let me get you both a coffee to warm up," the guy says, obviously noting the way Sawyer is drooling. "The name's Milo. Do you need any food or anything to get by?"

"No, we have everything we need. Maybe you and Buster want to join us."

"Nope, we're good here, aren't we, Buster?" He gives his dog's head a rub and Buster barks his response. "We want to be here in case anyone needs anything."

"Well, we're glad you stayed," Sawyer says as he pours coffee into two big paper cups. He puts plastic lids on them and hands them over as I take off my hat. His eyes narrow in on me. "Do I know you? You look familiar."

"Nope, not from around here. Just visiting."

"You sure as hell didn't pick a good time to visit," he ribs me with a laugh.

I tap my head. "Not too smart like that." That makes him laugh harder.

I take a big sip of coffee and Sawyer does the same. She frowns, and says, "I feel guilty for enjoying this when everyone is back at the motel freezing."

"Me too." I take another gulp. "Not guilty enough to keep me from enjoying it, though. We deserve it after going out in the cold. Besides with this gas, everyone will be able to have coffee when we get back." I put my arm around her and tug her to me. I'm not sure why. It's not like it's cold in here. Maybe I just like having her close.

"Right," she agrees, and drinks some more as she snuggles into me.

I turn to Milo. "Do you have gas cans we can borrow?"

"Got everything you need." He walks to one of the aisles and pulls a couple of brand new gas cans down. "Grab some more." Both Sawyer and I snatch up the big red cans. "You wait here while we fill them," I tell Sawyer.

Her head rears back, like I might be insane. "Are you crazy? I am not staying here alone with Killer."

"You don't like dogs?"

"I do, just not guard dogs, and Killer is eyeing me like I'm a big steak dinner."

I smile, liking that she likes animals. I don't know why that's important to me. Maybe it's because I want to go into animal science and I want everyone—her—to like animals as much as I do.

"Can you blame him?" I lean in and press my lips to hers. Honest to God, with the tip of her nose scarlet red, and her cheeks rosy from the cold, it's all I can do not to strip her and warm her properly. Tonight, though, that's exactly what I plan to do. My dick thickens at that thought, and I marshal him into submission for the time being. "You taste better than a steak dinner, and the name is Buster. He's just picking up on your fear. Animals sense anxiety."

"We can't all be dog whisperers like you."

"Are you sure I don't know you?" Milo pipes in. "You look so familiar."

It's true, I look a lot like my father, but I don't want to get into this conversation right now. As he eyes me, Sawyer takes a closer look at me and I tug on my toque, bringing it lower, almost to my eyes. "Nope, we better get these filled and head back," I say.

We follow Milo outside, get the snowmobile and cans filled and tie them down on the back of the sled. After we head inside and I pay, I shake his hand to thank him, give Buster a quick head rub, and head outside. I fix Sawyer's hat on her head, and make sure her zipper is all the way up before I gesture for her to get on the snowmobile. She doesn't move, instead she just stands there and looks at me.

"What?" I ask.

"Why does everyone think you're so familiar?"

I shrug and while I want to tell her who I really am and what I'm doing here, I'm afraid it could change things between us. I like getting to know each other like this. No pretending, just being who we really are. "I guess I have one of those faces."

"It's not a bad face," she says and crinkles up her nose.

I laugh. "Not a bad face? What's that supposed to mean?"

"It's not like you're a Hemsworth," she says, her lips quirking as she teases me.

"Oh, so you like the pretty boy look?"

She angles her head, her lips pursed in thought as she studies me. "I mean, your dimple is kind of cute, and your lips are nice and kissable." Her chest rises as she takes a deep breath. I take a deep breath too, remembering how much I loved my lips on her body last night.

I put my arm around her, and tug her to me. If we weren't wearing so many layers, she'd no doubt feel the erection growing between my legs. "We can stand here and freeze as we debate my qualities, or do you want to get back to the motel, get a hot shower, and let me show you what I can do with this mouth?"

Her eyes widen. "Yeah, that...that's what I want."

"Good, now get on."

SAWYER

I should be cold. Actually, I should be frozen half to death, but I'm not. Nope, with my arms around Chase, and my heart beating fast, it's keeping me warm from the top of my head to the tips of my toes. Okay well, my nose is cold, but that's it.

"Let me show you what I can do with this mouth."

As his words ping around in my lust-rattled brain, my entire body vibrates. Even if we ran out of gas, I probably could have shimmied us home with the way I'm trembling...with excitement. Although I have to admit, there is a part of me that's a bit nervous. I've never had sex before and I've seen what he has to work with. I laugh quietly, and don't even need to do the conversions from metric to standard, or rather vice versa, to know he just might ruin me.

He glances at me over his shoulder. "Something funny going on back there?"

I hug him a little tighter, and my heart skips as he puts a hand over mine and pats it. God, the last thing I'm going to do during this storm induced staycation is to let my emotions get involved. I've never been accused of being stupid and that's exactly what I would be if I let myself feel anything more for Chase.

"Nope, just happy we didn't have to walk back. I wasn't looking forward to piggybacking you. I prefer to keep my energy for other things."

He shakes his head and his hand moves to my knee to give it a squeeze. My insides quiver a little bit more. I really like Chase. Honestly how many men do I know that would go out in a storm to get gas because he was worried about the elderly? I'd say none, except my father—he's would go out in a storm for others—and it's true that I don't know or associate with many guys, but still... Chase seems to like me for me, and while he now knows I'm a theater nerd, he doesn't know that guys just aren't into me.

Screw you to the hockey players who always overlooked me. Deep down I know it's not just because of who my father is. My mother left because I wasn't enough, and hell, I never ever get the leading part in any of our school's productions. I guess I'm just not leading lady material. I try not to let it bother me, but sometimes, when the world is silent around me, it creeps into my thoughts and shatters the confidence I present to the world. Chase, however, seems to like me just for me, and the less he knows about my past the better.

I press my cheek against his back as the wind whips over us. I have his body to protect me from the cold, but he is going to be a popsicle by the time we get back. I'm looking forward to helping him thaw when we get to our room. Although it's going to take a long time to retrace. The tracks we took to get to the gas station are pretty much gone, having been blown in by the whirling snow. I'm beginning to think we might not get plowed out until our finals, in April. I hold him tight and try to keep him warm as he safely gets us back to the motel. He pulls up to the shed and kills the ignition. He climbs off and holds his hand out to help me.

"You go inside." The wind blows me around, and nearly carries his words away as he puts his hands on my shoulders to anchor me in place. "I don't want you getting carried to the top of the mountain in an updraft, so let me handle the gas and generator.."

"Want me to send Trev out?"

He glances at the motel and considers it a moment. "If he's not busy."

"Oh, he's probably busy," I tease. "But I'm sure he'll want to help you."

I turn to go, and he puts his arm around my waist, and tugs me back. "Thanks for keeping me company." I'm about to tell him no problem but he kisses me again. It's so weird. It's like he can't seem to keep his hands and lips off me, and I like that a lot. My gaze moves over his face as he tastes me deeply, and his arctic blue eyes turn almost transparent in the sunshine.

He breaks the kiss and his gaze moves to the tree line, heavy branches hang over a wide expanse of white. "What?" I ask and follow his gaze.

"Is that a lake, or a field?"

"A lake, why?"

There's a new, childlike excitement about him when he says, "We found those skates, remember?"

"That could be fun, or not. I haven't been on skates in forever. I'm not very good, to be honest." That's insane really, considering my father coaches hockey, and I've spent a lot of time at the rink over the years. I used to drool over the players when I was a pre-teen, but got tired of being ignored so I turned to reading, or writing, and other things to occupy myself until I was old enough that I didn't have to be dragged along to the rink anymore.

He rubs my arms. "I can help you."

"I don't know." I take in the amount of snow covering the ice. "It will have to be shoveled." I shake my head. "Where the hell is a Zamboni when you need one?"

"A what?"

"A Zamboni." I wave my hands, trying to find the best way to describe the machine. "You know, the thing that cleans and resurfaces the ice on a rink."

"Oh, I heard you and I know what it does. You just say it funny."

"I do not." I glare at him, feigning offence.

His features soften as he smiles, pulls one glove off and cups my cheek. "It's adorable the way you put your Canadian accent into it, though."

"Oh, okay," I say and lift my chin an inch, giving him a smile. "For the record, sometimes you have a Boston accent too."

"No, I don't."

"Sure you do. Remember when my cah went into the ditch, and you stopped your cah, and gave me a ride."

I laugh out loud. "I do not sound like that."

"Well, I guess we'll have to agree to disagree." I turn and give a little shake to my ass, his laugh following me as I head back inside. I get it, my backside is bundled up and that had to be the worst wiggle ever. But what I'm really thinking about is Chase staying in Nova Scotia. Is here really thinking about it?

Okay, girl, don't go there.

What's happening here is two people using each other to pass the time away. It is not a love affair, and I'm not looking for that anyway. I have a career to think about and he doesn't seem to even know what he wants to do with his life.

The motel is cool when I step inside, but still warmer than outdoors. I shake the snow off me and remove my toque and mitts. I head to the lobby and find Betsy sitting there in her big chair knitting, the sunlight slanting into the room, heating it.

"Sawyer," she says, her milky eyes brightening when she sees me. "You're back."

"And we have gas."

She claps her hands. "Oh, that is wonderful. Come in here, get out of the cold." She waves me over, and stands when I approach. She helps me out of my coat, and I grin at her motherly instincts. I had my grandmother, who was nurturing, but I don't think they reached my generation.

"I'm going to grab Trev to see if he can help Chase."

Betsy shakes my coat out when I get it off, and waves me on. I hurry upstairs, and listen for sound before I knock on Trev and Danielle's door. When I'm met with silence, I knock again, and a few seconds later the door swings open.

"We have gas." Wait, maybe that didn't come out quite right. "Chase is outside and wondering if you could help."

"On it." He leaves his door open as he goes for his coat and boots and I'm about to head to my room when Danielle invites me in. I'm reluctant at first. I don't want to invade their space and this is technically their honeymoon now.

"I don't want to bother you," I say as Trev moves past me and disappears down the stairs.

"Don't be silly. It's not like I have anything to do."

I step into their room, and note the mussed bed sheets. She starts fixing the sheets, and I notice her open suitcase with all the lingerie inside. I wouldn't know a sexy piece of lingerie if it was choking me. She must notice me staring.

She steps up to the suitcase, and pulls out a few things, the tags still on them. She holds up a cute red, one-piece number and puts it against my body. "I think this would look much better on you than me."

I wave my hands. "Oh, no. I can't wear this."

She grins. "Why not. Your suitcase is still in your car, isn't it?" She looks the lingerie over. "This was a gift, but it's not really my style. I think it would be gorgeous on your body, though."

"Really?"

She chuckles. "If you don't believe me, wear it tonight and see how Chase reacts."

I touch the silky fabric as my mind goes on an erotic adventure. I've never worn anything like this in my life, but this trip is all about being someone different, right?

"Are you sure?"

"I insist."

Just then the lights flicker and we both hold our breath. They go off and come on again, this time staying on.

Danielle claps her hands. "Thank God, I am desperate for a shower and a coffee."

"Same here," I say and hold the lingerie close to my chest. "Thanks for this, Danielle." I'm about to head to my room but turn back and tell her, "Chase and I found some fun stuff in the attic. Vintage clothes, and skates. Do you guys want to skate later maybe?"

"That would be so much fun. Trev plays hockey. Maybe we can find some sticks and have a fun game."

Hockey, yuck.

"Sure, I'll check with Chase." I squeeze the lingerie. "Thanks again for this."

I hurry back to my room, leaving the door unlocked for Chase as I tuck the lingerie into a drawer, a secret for later. Boots in the hall announce his arrival. I wait, but hear only Trev entering their room. What happened to Chase? I go to the window to look out, but he's nowhere to be found.

Old insecurities creep into my brain. Has he had enough of me already and decided he doesn't want to room with me anymore? Did he snowmobile out to the main road and hitch a ride to the city? Was the lingerie a waste of my time, simply wishful thinking?

As my mind races, I take a deep breath and as I let it out, I let my worries go with it. I'm being ridiculous. He couldn't keep his hands or mouth off me earlier. Chances are he's probably still fiddling with the generator. I try to busy myself, checking my phone before it dies completely, but I still can't get a signal, and running the tap in the sink, hoping that somehow speeds up the heating of the water. It doesn't.

Growing restless, I leave my room and head to the café. I make a pot of coffee, and fill two paper cups, ready to take them back to the room when something or someone touches my neck. I'm about to scream, toss the coffee in the air and run, because I'm sure some gigantic spider escaped the attic and is now loose in the motel—or maybe the place really is haunted—when Chase's voice hushes me.

"Easy, Sawyer, it's just me." His hands go to my hips, and he presses against me. I'm pretty sure that's not a flashlight in his pocket.

"You scared me," I say, breathlessly, but now it's not from fear. Nope, not from fear at all. What is it about this guy that turns me into a dim-witted moth? I've seen plenty of hot guys in my life. But none of them have ever touched me, or looked at me the way Chase does, and I loved the openness and honesty between us last night. "I thought you were a spider, or a ghost."

He chuckles. "Sorry, I just saw you standing here and you looked so good, I needed a taste." His cool lips land on the side of my neck and I moan as his mouth warms from my body heat.

He breaks the kiss and I spin, taking in the heat in his eyes. "Where were you?"

He frowns, worry moving into his eye as he gazes at me. "Is everything okay?"

"Yeah, sure." I try for casual. Lord, he doesn't need to know I was worried he'd changed his mind about me. "I heard Trev come back and was worried about you."

"Aww, you were worried." He produces the dimple that drives me a little crazy, but he's hedging, not really telling me where he was. What doesn't he want me to know? "That's so sweet."

"It's cold and windy out there, and there are wild animals on these mountains."

"Wild animals, huh. Like what, the Canadian beaver?" His voice is light and teasing as he grins at me.

"Well, yes, but there are other animals too, like coyotes and bears."

"Aren't the bears hibernating?"

"I don't know. Maybe the storm woke them. You could have been eaten alive."

"Eaten alive, eh?" he asks as he slides his hands down my back, cupping my ass and aligning his erection with my sex.

"And you should never underestimate the beaver, Chase. If trapped or cornered, it will attack. They can be quite dangerous."

His hand slides between my legs and he strokes me through the big sweatpants hanging low on my hips. "Yeah?"

"Yeah. They used to be endangered, you know, due to over-hunting for their thick fur." God, what am I saying? His hand lingers between my legs, and I shamelessly move my hips, encouraging him to touch me before I melt into a puddle at his feet.

"Thick fur, huh?" he grins, and that's when I get it. We're talking about beavers, but not the ones recognized as the emblem of Canada. "I didn't realize Canadian beavers weren't like other beavers."

"I guess you have a thing or two to learn," I say, with a lift of my chin, even though I'm a hot mess inside as he toys with me. His fingers go to the string holding the big sweatpants on my hips and he lightly toys with it. I moan, my body sizzling from the inside out. If I had panties on, they'd be soaked, but since I didn't have any clean ones, I opted to go commando.

"Do they have any natural predators?"

"Sure, coyotes, foxes, bobcats..."

"These predators, they eat the beavers."

Ohmigod.

"Yes," I croak out as he dips his hand into the sweatpants, and slides it low.

"You're not wearing..."

"I didn't have any clean ones and we were going for a long snowmobile ride and—"

"You can't go for a ride without clean panties," he murmurers.

Something in the way he says panties, and everything in the way he's looking at me lets me know that he's the predator and I'm the prey when he gets me alone, I'm the one who's going to be eaten alive. I put my hands on his shoulders and hang on because I'm sure it's going to be one hell of a wild ride.

11

CHASE

Betsy steps into the kitchen and we break apart. "Chase, thank you so much for getting the generator going. You're a sweet boy." She walks up to him and cups his cheeks and my stupid heart misses a beat. "Malcolm was so happy to hear you got it running. He's not much into mechanical things, and I've been meaning to call in a repair man for years now."

"Did Malcolm have any news on plowing?"

She shakes her head. "Afraid not. But I told him we were doing okay. The guests all had a good breakfast and are resting now."

"Would you mind if we borrowed the skates in the attic?" I ask.

"Help yourself to whatever you need."

Sawyer glances at me. "Danielle talked about playing hockey." I scan Sawyer's face, and she doesn't seem too pleased by the idea.

"We don't have to do that," I say.

"Do you play hockey?"

Okay, I can't lie. Well, I can but I'm not going to. "Yeah," I tell her. "I play."

"I figured."

My body tenses and I try to appear relaxed. "Why do you say that?"

"You look athletic. I bet you play all kinds of sports."

"Everything except curling." I snap my finger, pretending to be disappointed. "Too bad you didn't have any rocks. You could have taught me."

"I actually have a couple in my car. I bought them at a garage sale and keep them in my trunk for weight, like sandbags, in the winter. Maybe I'll go get them," she says, and I laugh. She touches my nose. "Careful what you wish for, Chase."

Betsy walks to a cupboard and opens it. "If you're going to shovel off the lake and have a game, maybe you'll want to build a fire and make s'mores. There's a fire pit and logs to sit on, but you'll have to shovel them out."

"There's a lot of dry wood in the shed," I say.

"Lots of paper here to help you get it going." She points to a stack of paper on the counter. She winks. "The secret to a good fire is firestarter." I follow her gaze and see the big can near the back of the café door. "That'll really give you a big blaze. Just be sure to dress warm."

Sawyer eyes me. "Sound like fun?" I ask her. She nods and I add, "It will give us something to do to pass the time until the water heats up."

"There are shovels in the shed," Betsy tells us, but I'd spotted them earlier.

"Seems like you two are conspiring against me," Sawyer laughs. She hands me two cups of coffee, and fills two more cups. "I hope Danielle and Trev like their coffee black."

We head down the hall and Betsy goes back to her comfy chair as we go up the stairs. With our hands full, I use my elbow to knock on our neighbor's door, and Danielle flings it open. "Sawyer, you're a saint. Hot water and now coffee."

"You have hot water already?"

"Warm," she says. "Enough to sponge bath."

Sawyer nods toward me. "We were thinking of clearing the lake, going for a skate and making a bonfire. Are you guys in?"

"Yeah, we're in," Trev says, opening the door and accepting the coffee.

"We'll meet you down there then," Sawyer tells them, and I hand over her cup of coffee and open our bedroom door. She steps in and squeals when she sees her suitcase, and her two curling rocks.

"Chase!" She turns and stares at me.

"That's where I was. I went to your car to get your things." I shrug, my brain going back to when I disappeared for a half hour and how it seemed to have rattled her. Did she think I left on the snowmobile or something, and abandoned them all? "I wanted to surprise you. Something tells me you don't like surprises, though."

She gazes at me with genuine thanks, and I can't help but think my buddy was right and Canadians are honest, genuine people. "That was so nice of you."

"What can I say?" I joke. "I must be turning into a Canadian, eh?"

"You can use our lingo, but you can't call yourself a true Canadian until you've curled."

"So many rules," I groan. "I was thinking you could teach me how at some point."

"Sure, and you should be grateful you're not in Newfoundland. There you'd have to kiss a cod."

"I'd rather kiss you." I pull her to me for a kiss. Her mouth is warm, and pliable, and my dick thickens, wanting to take her here and now, hard and fast. I won't. I want her first time to be better than me going at her like a horny teen getting a glimpse of his first boob. Been there and fucked that up. I cringe at the memory, and like to think I've grown and learned some new moves.

A knock comes on our door, and we break apart. "Can you get that? I need a second."

She chuckles as I adjust my pants, moving to the window to tame my erection. Why am I always so hard around her? Maybe it's because the pressure is off and I can relax for once, or maybe it's because I really like her. She pulls open the door to find Danielle and Trev all bundled up and ready to hit the ice.

"Come grab a pair that fits," I say, having gathered the box of skates and four hockey sticks from the attic after I collected Sawyer's things from her car.

We all root through the box, and once we're all dressed, we make our way outside, fortunately, the wind is starting to die down a bit. With a brand new can of lighter fluid in my pocket for the fire, I hand the sticks to the girls, grab two shovels from the shed and pass them to Trev so I can grab an armload of dry wood and tinder.

"Are there more shovels in there?" Sawyer asks. "I'm not useless."

"I am," Danielle teases. She holds her mittens out. "I don't want to ruin this brand-new manicure."

"We got this." Trev says, and kisses his wife. "I don't want you to ruin your nails, either."

Trev and I trek ahead and I glance behind me to find Sawyer and Danielle treading in our big footsteps, making the walk through the deep snow a bit easier for them.

"Keep an eye out for beavers," I yell back. "I hear they can be ferocious." Both Danielle and Trev give me an odd look and I explain, "I'm from Boston, and Sawyer warned me about dangerous Canadian beavers." I meet Sawyer's glance and she looks like she's about to murder me, but I like the little secrets we share.

Danielle nudges Sawyer. "What's that all about?"

Sawyer shakes her head. "I'll explain later."

I stifle a laugh, as we reach the lake, the heavy trees hanging overhead, snow falling from the bowed branches. "Why don't you girls make a snowman?" Trev suggests. "We'll dig out the fire pit, then clear the ice."

Sawyer frowns and crosses her arms like a petulant child. "I'd rather make a sandman."

"Same," Danielle agrees. "But a snowman will have to be the next best thing."

As the girls start rolling up balls of snow, Trev and I get to work on finding and clearing the fire pit. Once it's done, we get a roaring fire going to warm us up, then slip into the skates and begin clearing the ice.

"Do you think you'll still be able to make your honeymoon?"

"I'm not too sure. We'll probably have to reschedule." He digs his shovel into the snow, throws his arms over it and rests his chin on his hands. "She's making the best of it, but I know she's disappointed. Hell, I am too. We saved for a long time for this."

I nod, and glance at the girls. I found a shit ton of things in the attic. Maybe there's a way we can make up for them missing their trip. "I have an idea," I say to Trev.

"What's that?" He begins to shovel again, and I follow beside him. Before I can tell him what I have in mind, a big dollop of snow lands on my head. "Jesus." The wet snow drips into my face and I brush it away as I glance at the low hanging tree branches. The sun must be melting the snow.

I move away from the tree, but Trev isn't quick enough. "What the hell?" he mutters. I turn to find him brushing snow off the front of his coat. I point upward.

"We're under the hanging trees." Just then a big ball of snow hits me right in the face and a shriek comes from the girls. I sputter and spit, and look to where the girls are building a snowman. They both quickly look away, and that's when I realize it was them throwing snowballs at us.

"You're going to pay for that," I yell.

"What?" Sawyer calls back innocently, but it's easy to tell she's trying not to laugh. I shake my head. When was the last time I felt like a kid, without a million responsibilities weighing down my shoulders, the pressure to succeed and perform is always in the forefront of my brain? I'm not sure, but I like it.

"Don't play cute," I say, even though I like how cute she is just playing around. It's nice to see her have fun, and the fact that she was on her way to Florida, searching for a fast hook-up, is a good indication that she could use a break from real life too.

"Fine then, it's payback for letting me wear that house dress." I laugh as she goes back to the snowman, the two of them struggling to get the snowman's head on properly. I drop my shovel, skate across the ice and help them. Once I get it positioned, they fill the cracks in with snow.

"See, snow isn't so bad after all," I say.

"It's not the beach," Sawyer mumbles, but she's smiling as she admires her snowman.

"No, but if we sit by the fire and eat s'mores and close our eyes maybe we can pretend it's summertime. Beside you told me you made the best s'mores and I'm dying for a bite." I lean into her, and nip at her nose with my teeth.

She laughs and pushes me away. "Did you get the marshmallows?"

"I got them," Trev says, and points to the backpack he dropped by the fire. We all make our way to the fire, and I brush the blowing snow off the logs before we sit. Sawyer wiggles in her seat.

"This is kind of cozy." She glances around, pulls out her phone and takes a few pictures of the lake, fire, our new friends, and me. She tries to take a couple more and frowns. "Dead."

"Same," Danielle agrees. "I would have loved to make a TikTok, or at least posted something on Insta."

"Me too," Sawyer says. "I did get a few pics, though. I'll get your number later and send them to you." She holds her hands over the flames. "Do we have sticks for roasting?"

"We have hockey sticks," I tell her.

"That's a good use for them," she shoots back.

Laughing,

I walk up to a tree, snap off a couple of spindly branches and hand them out. "How about these instead?"

Sawyer puts a marshmallow on the end of her stick. "Prepare to be amazed." Danielle begins eating the chocolate as Trev roasts a couple marshmallows.

"God, this is good." Danielle hands me the bar and I take a bite, and put a piece in Sawyer's mouth.

"Delicious," she says, and when the marshmallow is done, she puts a piece of chocolate on it and squeezes two graham crackers around it, until the marshmallow is oozing out. "That's the trick to making them gourmet." She holds it out for me and I take a big bite.

"Fine dining at its best," Danielle says and squishes her own marshmallow between the graham crackers. "Everything tastes better in the outdoors."

Sawyer gives me another bite, and it's weird how intimate it feels just sharing a sugary treat with her. I shift a bit closer and she smiles at me. "Not so bad, eh?"

"Not bad at all, Chase, and you used eh correctly this time. Maybe you'll make a good Canadian after all."

Something in the way she says my name sends my imagination into overdrive, and I sit here eating marshmallows while I envision my name on her lips as I bury my face between her legs. While I want her sexually, there's something else, something strange going on inside me. I simply like being with her. She's fun, and open, and doesn't care about makeup or hat hair. I don't think I've ever met a more 'real' woman in my life. I think my folks would really like her.

Whoa, where did that come from? It's not like I'm going to bring her home to meet my parents. I'm sure after this weekend we'll never see each other. She might be a theatre student at Scotia Academy, but it's a big college and we obviously travel in different circles. There's no chance she'd show up at a hockey game, not when she hates hockey so much.

"Something on your mind, Chase?" she asks. Her voice is light, but that lightness doesn't reach her eyes.

"Yeah, I was thinking about how messy you are when you eat."

"I am not messy," she shoots back around a big mouthful of marshmallow." I laugh, and wipe chocolate from the side of her face.

I hold my finger out to show her the streak of chocolate. "See, messy." I put my finger into my mouth and lick it, and she swallows hard, a new kind of heat in her eyes. As my stupid cock thickens, I look for a distraction.

"So why did you two get married in December?" I ask Danielle and Trev. "Isn't June the month for weddings?"

"We both have been so busy with our careers, working day and night to make a name for ourselves, and I thought, if we wait for the right time, it might never come and we could be waiting forever, so we dropped everything and got married."

Sawyer smiles. "That's pretty insightful."

"We have to enjoy the journey, right?" Danielle says. "Our destination was Jamaica, but this is our journey to get there, and we're going to enjoy it."

"I like that," I murmur quietly. I've had my head down, barely dating, working hard to get the grades and the goals on the ice so I can make it to the NHL. I almost forget what fun was like and I suspect the same has happened for Sawyer.

So far, since I've been stranded here, I've been spending more time enjoying the journey and less time worrying about the destination. When our time here together ends, will that change, will we part ways and go back to our regularly scheduled lives? Or is it possible that we can pick up where we left off here, and build a future together? I haven't known her very long, and I'm a little shocked at the off-the-beaten path my thoughts have wandered, but I can't deny that I'm suddenly thinking about what life would be like with her in it.

Then again, maybe my brain is frozen out here in the cold, in the middle of nowhere, where beavers attack, and I'm just not thinking clearly.

12

SAWYER

Since nighttime comes early in December, it's pretty much pitch black when we finish on the ice and head inside. "Please tell me the water is hot enough for a shower?" I say, my body trembling from the cold. I was having far too much fun to call it quits, and while I sucked on skates and probably have a dozen bruises on my backside, I did manage to score on Chase.

Something tells me he let me. He was a pro out there on the ice, handling the hockey stick like it was an extension of himself. Like he said, he played all sports—except curling—and there's no denying he's fit and athletic. Wouldn't my dad just love a guy like him on the team. Personally, I wouldn't want him around any of those egotistical jerks who lay down bets and play games with women's bodies and hearts.

"It should be. Once we all get showered, and this place is warm, I'll turn the generator off for the night so we can conserve gas." He taps my backside to set me into motion and I wince. "Oh, sorry," he says and cups my face. He looks so thoroughly upset, I grin.

"It's okay. I'll live."

"I promise to kiss all your sore spots better," he murmurs into my ear.

Trev rolls his eyes. "All right, you two get a room."

"You head up. I'll let Betsy know the plan so she can prepare the guests for no electricity tonight."

I nod, hating to admit that I like the idea of fumbling around in the dark with him.

"Tell her after I get warmed up, I'll cook dinner for everyone," Danielle says.

"Thanks Danielle. I'm sure she'll appreciate that."

Danielle and Trev kick snow from their boots and take off their toques and mitts as they head back to their room. I'm about to follow them when Chase tugs me back to him. I collide with his body, and he dips his head. "That was fun," he says.

I smile up at him and I'm not sure what's different, but something has changed, it's subtle but I can sense it. His blue eyes move over my face adoringly, and it does the strangest things to my heart. It beats a little faster and I swear to God if it starts getting involved in this snowed-in fling, we're going to have words. "I'll be right up. Go up and get warm."

"I'm not sure I'll ever be warm again."

"I'll take that bet," he says, and that one word sets off alarm bells inside me and triggers bad locker room memories.

"What?" I ask, my muscles tightening as fight or flight instinct kicks in. When I overheard the bet in the locker room, I fled.

"Hey." His voice is soft and low as he brushes his knuckles over my face. "Are you okay?"

"Yeah, I just...what were you saying?"

"I was saying I bet I can make you warm."

"Oh," I murmur. "Are you a betting kind of guy?"

He nods. "If the stakes are high enough, I am."

I'm not in the locker room anymore and this is Chase I'm with, not some egotistical jock. Chase doesn't know the guys on the team used to bet on who could 'bag' me. Apparently, there was a lot of money in the coffers, going to whichever team member had the balls to follow through with the bet. I guess no one needed the money badly enough, as if they'd had a chance with me anyway. I know what they're all like and I've seen them turn on the charm—with other girls. I prided myself on being too smart to fall for it. Not that any of them ever tried.

"It's on," I say, looking forward to discovering how he plans to warm me.

He grins. "Head on up, and I'll go find Betsy."

I watch him go, and dammit, he looks as good going as he does coming. Speaking of coming...a little gasp catches in my throat as my mind relives the way he ejaculated on my breasts. Damn that was sexy, and what the hell is going on with me? I don't think about things like that. Ah, but here in the middle of nowhere, where I can be anyone or anything I want...I do think about things like that.

I hurry up the stairs to our room and open the door. We didn't even bother locking it when we left earlier, partly because we're in Nova Scotia and many in rural communities leave their doors unlocked, and partly because no one here looks like they're about to steal anything. I remove my coat and boots and rush to the bathroom to check for hot water. I let loose a sigh as the warmth splashes over my skin and makes it a bit itchy. My focus turns to the shower. Maybe I should jump in now, so it's free for when Chase gets back.

Deciding to do just that, I close the bathroom door, pull the plastic shower curtain across the ancient yellow tub, and turn on the water. As it warms, I climb out of my sweats and climb in. The spray hits my cold skin and it burns at first, but as I warm up, it starts feeling glorious. I moan as I put my head completely under, and let the water fall over my body.

My lids fly open at the sound of the shower curtain crinkling. "Did you start without me?"

My first reaction is to cover my naked body. "Chase, you scared me."

"I seem to be doing that a lot. Sorry."

I grin. "Look at you, apologizing all the time now. Yeah, you're definitely becoming Canadian."

His gaze leaves my face, and travels down my bare body. "Why are you covering yourself?"

I remove my arm from across my breasts and my other hand from my sex. "I don't know."

"You know I've seen you naked, right?"

"I know."

As my hands dangle by my sides, he growls with approval. My pulse jumps, and I have to say I love the adoration in his eyes as he takes in my body.

"That's better." He begins to peel his clothes from his body.

While I'm absolutely taking pleasure in his hard nakedness, I ask, "What do you think you're doing?"

"Joining you." I angle my head, admiring his muscles. "I walked in here and heard you moaning. I thought you might need a hand."

"I wasn't...you know."

He grins. "Can't say it?" he teases.

"Touching myself," I blurt out.

"What's that?" he asks as he climbs in and fixes the curtain. "You want me to help you touch yourself?"

"That's not..." My words fall off as he takes my hand and places it between my legs. He pushes one of my fingers inside me, and slides his in right with it. "Ohmigod," I murmur. "Chase..."

"You like that, babe?"

"I...do." He works both of our fingers inside my tight pussy, and it's all I can do to remain standing. "I've never..."

"Showered with a guy before."

"Right."

"Never had your and a guy's fingers in your sweet pussy at the same time."

Oh my God, that feels so good. "That too."

He moves his hand, so the heel is pressed against my clit. Every time he touches me, it gets better and better. Cripes, I hope we never get plowed out. My free hand seeks out his cock, and he's missile hard as I grip him. He groans and I love the way he reacts to my touch.

"I've never done this in the shower before either." He pumps our fingers in and out of my hot pussy, and I can barely keep my focus on pleasuring him. My hand falls and I fumble to find his cock again as need hits me like a whip, right between my legs. I can barely think, barely breathe as my body quakes all over.

"I want...I need...Chase, your cock," is all I manage to get out as my throat dries. I take deep gasping breaths.

"I want you to come, baby. You can touch my cock, and do whatever the hell you want with it later. Right now, I just want your cum all over me."

God, are all guys this considerate? After listening to the antics in the guy's locker room, I somehow doubt it, but I can't question such things right now, not when pressure is building, raining down on me like the hot water from the nozzle.

I grip his shoulders, and he steps closer, his mouth going to my neck. He lightly bites my skin, no doubt leaving little love bruises. Not love, this isn't love. This is sex. Jeez, I can't even think straight.

"You needed this, huh?" he asks as light spasms tug at our fingers.

"Yes...God yes."

"This whole time we were outside, were you thinking about my cock, and all the things I was going to do to you when I got you alone?"

"Uh huh," I manage to get out as my words begin to fail me. "All day...it was...like...one long foreplay session."

He chuckles. "Agreed and I've been thinking about you too. My cock has been so hard for you." My stomach flutters. I love that he's been thinking about me the same way I've been thinking about him. "Later, when I get you on our bed, I'm going to put my mouth on this sweet pussy and eat you alive, Sawyer. I'm going to bury my face in your hot little cunt, and then when you're nice and wet and quivering all over, and begging for more, I'm going to fill you with my cock."

I claw at his skin as he lays out the night's events, fueling my body and my imagination. "But first, I'm going to put you on your knees, and you're going to take me into your mouth."

"Ohmigod, Chase."

"You want that, Sawyer? You want my cock in your mouth? You want to taste me?"

"I do," I cry as his fingers hit the bundle of nerves inside me perfectly, and I explode all over our fingers. Hot juices spill from my body and sizzle down my hand, and his groan of pleasure bounces off the tiled walls. I can't believe I spent so many years missing out on this kind of pleasure.

As my body quivers, and I find it harder and harder to stand, I cling to Chase. He eases his finger from my body, and wraps his arms around me. "I got you," he whispers, and places me directly under the warm spray. He reaches for the soap on the ledge, and begins to lather my body. His fingers glide over my breasts and he groans.

"I've not spent enough time here," he murmurs, his hard cock pressing against my side. "I plan to rectify that."

A laugh bubbles out of my throat, not a worry in the world as this man takes care of me. I touch his chest, enjoy the play of his muscles beneath my fingers, and I can't wait until I can put my mouth on him.

After he washes me, I let the water rinse the soap away as he quickly cleans himself. The water begins to turn a bit cooler by the time we turn it off. He slides the curtain open and grabs a big fluffy towel from the racks. He wraps it around me.

"Warm?"

"No," I fib.

"Damn, I'll have to keep on trying. I'm competitive and I plan to win the bet."

"You can try but I have no idea how you're going to get me warm. It looks like the hot water tanks are emptying and when the generator is turned off, this place will cool down fast."

"I do like a challenge," he says as he knots his towel around his waist. I yelp as he scoops me up and carries me to the bed. He gently tosses me down and I push my suitcase off, the contents spilling all over the carpet as he goes to the curtains to pull them closed.

"We don't need any wildlife watching us."

"Ah, you've heard about our voyeuristic Canadian beavers, have you?"

He laughs, hard, and slides in beside me. "Babe, this is the only beaver I'm interested in squaring off against tonight. Now that I've gotten a taste, I can't seem to get enough." He lightly pets my sex, and I grin at his bad joke as my legs slide open to give him access.

His mouth finds mine, and his kiss is soft, leisurely, as he savours the depths of my mouth and moans like I'm the sweetest thing he's ever tasted. He rolls on top of me, pinning me with his weight, and I wrap my legs around him. His rock-hard cock presses against my pubic bone as he moves against me, a desperate need about him.

With every ounce of strength I possess, I push him off me, and he rolls to the side, worry all over his face as he gazes at me.

"Sawyer?" He watches me, transfixed as I climb off the bed. "I'm sorry...I thought—"

"I thought this is what we were doing first." His words fall off and he gulps as I drop to my knees, open my mouth in invitation and crook my fingers, gesturing for him to come to me.

"Fuck me," he moans.

His cock is thick and hard as he closes the distance, and I lay out my tongue, asking for his cock without words. He grips my hair, his eyes laser focused as he moves his hips forward and feeds me his cock. I relax my jaw as his girth stretches my lips, and his groan of pleasure swirls through me as he pistons into my waiting mouth. I moan around his cock as he fucks me with it, and my body begins to warm all over, arousal sharpening between my legs.

His grip on my hair tightens as he thickens even more in my mouth, and I reach up and cup his balls. "I want to stay right here, all night..." He grunts as I suck harder. "But baby, I need to be inside your pussy. I've thought about it all day."

He jerks his hips back and plops from my mouth. I pout in disappointment and glance up at him, as he wipes the saliva off my face with the tip of his finger.

"I wasn't done," I murmur.

He pulls me to my feet, and kisses me as his hands go around to my ass to lift me onto his hips. "You like sucking my cock, Sawyer?"

"Yes. I like it, and I wanted to make you come, and see if I like that."

His jaw clenches like my words are pure torture. "You want to learn a lot of things, huh?"

"I do."

He reaches between my legs, and slides a finger in me. "But baby, if you keep sucking, you're going to make me come, and I thought you wanted me in here tonight?"

"I do," I say a measure of excitement and nervousness gripping me.

His gaze moves over my face. "You're sure?"

"Positive." I sound anxious—maybe even a little desperate—and there's no hiding it, not from him.

"Are you nervous?"

"A little," I admit. "But I'm in good hands."

He goes still for a minute, my words surprising him. I cup his face and kiss him softly. "Yeah, you are," he murmurs into my mouth as he turns and walks me toward the bed, stepping over my suitcase and spilled clothes. That's when I remember the lingerie. I guess it will have to wait for next time.

Next time.

Hell yeah, there's going to be a next time. I plan to 'get it gurl' until the last of the snow is removed.

He gently lays me on the bed, and falls over me. He kisses my mouth, my chin, and moves to my neck. I moan when he hits the sensitive spot that sends heat to my sex. He presses hot, open-mouthed kisses to my flesh, going lower until he finds my breasts. I grip his hair, much the same way he gripped mine when he had his cock in my mouth, and hold him to me. He licks and sucks and gently bites them, and I writhe beneath him. It didn't take him long to figure out my likes and dislikes and as far as I can tell, he's liked everything I've done to him so far.

His mouth goes to my sex, and he licks lightly all the way from the bottom to the top, taking a moment to circle my clit with his tongue. I moan, my hips coming off the bed as my nerve endings fire.

"Chase," I murmur.

He mumbles, "I love the taste of you."

I cup my breasts and tease my nipples as pleasure gathers in my core and radiates outward. I move against his tongue, my body warming all over.

His head lifts, his eyes meeting mine, like he's checking in with me. "More," I beg without hesitation.

He bends to give me one last lick before climbing up my body. He brushes my hair back, his cock pressing against my leg. "I need to get a condom."

Breathless, I nod eagerly. "Okay,"

"Don't go anywhere," he says, like my legs could actually hold my weight.

He hurries off the bed and searches his pants. He grumbles something and dumps the contents of his suitcase. Frustration dances in his eyes and he grips a fistful of hair at the back of his neck as he glances at me. "Jesus Christ, I don't have a condom. I thought I had one in my pants or at least my bag."

Something weird tugs at my heart. I guess he's not the type of guy to walk around with a box of condoms, screwing everything in sight. The guys on my dad's team wouldn't be caught dead without protection.

"My suitcase," I say quickly, about to scramble off the bed, when he bends and picks up a brand-new box from my open bag. I almost laugh. He's not the type of guy to carry condoms around but apparently, I am.

His grin is wicked. "I like a girl who's prepared." I smile, but the truth is, I could never be prepared for a guy like him. I was hoping to hook up with someone random, not some guy I'm snowed in with. A guy who is fun, and spontaneous, and cares about others. No, a guy like that might find his way into my heart and I'd be really stupid if I let that happen.

Don't be stupid, Sawyer!

He rips into the box, pulls out a condom and with deft hands that have done the deed many times, he sheathes himself. I study his hard, cut body, the way his muscles ripple as he climbs onto the bed, and moves between my legs.

"You okay, Sawyer?" he asks as he flattens himself out, bracing his arms on the bed beside me, to adjust his weight.

"I am," I say, and lift up to kiss his mouth. I don't want to worry about falling for him, or what a future without his hands on me might look like. Right now, I just want to feel him inside me and enjoy all the pleasure I know his body is going to give me. I rake my hands through his hair and settle back on my pillow. "Chase," I whisper as he moves his hips to position himself.

"Yeah?" He goes still, and I like the way he's not in a hurry to just fuck me.

There's a tightness in my throat when I admit, "I'm glad it's you."

Something passes over his face, something warm, and sincere...something that cradles my heart and warns I could be in trouble.

Careful, Sawyer.

"Yeah?

"Yeah, I know we're still strangers, but I think I know a little about you. I like what I know and that makes it better than a random hookup."

"It does, doesn't it," he says, and his mouth captures mine for a kiss so deep and tender, one would think this was about more than sex. His cock presses against my entrance, and he hesitates for a second. I lift my hips, letting him know exactly what I want. He inches in a bit, and I take a deep breath, prepared for a little pain.

"Doing okay?" he asks, and lifts his head. Our eyes meet and lock and I nod my head. He pushes in an inch more, and I moan as he stretches me open.

"More," I whisper, and lift for him again. He powers forward and in one hard thrust he's inside me. I open my mouth and no sound forms as pain and pleasure blend and tear through me.

"I'm inside, babe," he says, kissing my mouth, and cheeks and nose as his body stills, like he's giving me time to get used to the fullness. "I'm deep inside and you feel so good."

"I feel every inch of you, and I love what I feel."

He moves slowly, inching out a tiny bit and gliding back in. I moan and grip his shoulders, holding tight as he fucks me. His body shifts, the angle hitting differently as he slides a hand between our bodies and applies pressure to my clit.

"Yes," I cry out. I rock with him, his cock easily gliding in and out now, and within no time at all, pleasure overcomes my entire being.

"You like that?" he asks.

"I do. More...just like that."

We move together, instinct taking over. I always thought my first time would be clumsy and awkward, and it might have been if it wasn't with Chase. His breathing changes, so does mine, as he shifts his body, altering the pace and rhythm. His eyes remain on my face, as he continually gauges my reactions. God, he is so incredibly sweet.

A wave of pleasure steals my breath, and beads of moisture break out on my skin as my body temperature jumps and I know exactly what's happening. "Chase," I cry as his cock takes me higher and higher until I'm tumbling over the cliff, freefalling into a glorious orgasm that makes me forget a world exists beyond this room.

"Jesus," he grunts as I clench around his pistoning cock. "That's it, come all over my cock." I glance at him, see the pride mixed with pleasure in his eyes. He's happy he made this good for me, and I'm happy that he cares.

He pushes deep and goes still as my body stops clenching. He gulps air. "I'm there, babe."

"Let me feel it."

He grunts and buries his face in my neck as he lets go. He holds the side of my face and I close my eyes, concentrating on each hard pulse inside my body. I love everything about this. His breath is hot on my skin as he breathes deep, and while he might be inside me, I love the intimacy in the way he's holding me. He stops spasming, and he puts one hand on my hips as he inches out. He cups my sex with his big hand, and the warmth from his palm seeps through my blood and wraps around my heart.

"Are you warm, babe?"

"Hot," I murmur, my heart pounding, heat firing through my blood as he gets rid of the condom, snuggles in next to me, covers us with the blanket.

His grin is playful as he tucks my hair behind my ear and says,

"Looks like I won the bet."

I chuckle, as he presses kisses to my cheek. "You won," I agree with a laugh. With every contest, there's usually a winner and a loser, and while I feel I won here too, the man touched me with tender hands as I gave him my virginity— I'm more worried about losing something I have no intentions of losing. Something that's pounding far too hard in my chest.

13

CHASE

Morning sunlight slanting into the room pulls me awake and I turn to find the other side of the bed empty. I jackknife up, and take a moment to examine the strange burst of emptiness that I shouldn't be feeling. It's true, I don't usually do sleepovers and always wake up in my own bed. I prefer it that way. Okay, correction. I used to prefer it that way. Yesterday morning, I loved waking up and finding Sawyer here, glancing out the window. She might not have been in the bed, but she was here with me.

Pipes squeal in the bathroom and my heart settles as my gaze flies to the closed door. I stretch out, my pulse doing a happy dance as I climb to my feet, and look down at my bare-ass body. The chill that invaded the motel overnight falls over me and I tug on my jeans, nearly tripping over Sawyer's open suitcase. I note a pile of stapled papers, and steal a fast glance at the bathroom door. Why does she have a stack of papers? Would it be wrong to look? An invasion of her privacy? Yeah, it would be.

Pushing down my curiosity, I tug on a T-shirt and my heart jumps into my throat as the bathroom door creaks open and I turn to find Sawyer standing there. She's in a T-shirt and pajama shorts. Obviously, what she'd packed to sleep in for her trip.

"Good morning."

"Morning." Her eyes are half-lidded, a small, satisfied smile on her face.

"Come here."

I drop down onto the edge of the bed, and widen my legs. She comes to stand between them, and I put my hand between her legs and lightly touch her. I don't miss her little intake of breath, or my thickening cock.

"Are you sore?"

"A little." She leans forward, her long mess of dark hair falling over her shoulders and framing her gorgeous face. She's not just gorgeous, she's also really sweet. "But it's not a bad sore. It reminds me of last night."

My cock thickens more at the reminder of last night. Not that I hadn't been thinking of it. Sawyer might have been looking for some random guy to take her virginity, and while I really am that to her, I care about her. I wanted her first time to be as special as I could make it. She deserves that.

Voices from the hall reach our ears. "Looks like everyone is waking up." The chatter grows louder and more jovial, and she lifts her brow. "Maybe they have news on the plow. Perhaps we're getting out of here today."

I put my hands on her hips and she blinks rapidly. "That would be great." It's a lie and I must be crazy since I'm not excited to leave. But she might still make it to Florida. "Do you think you can still catch a flight?" I ask, hope in my voice.

"That ship has sailed." She chuckles. "Or rather, that plane has flown."

"Bummer."

"And I have my car to deal with. I don't even know if it's drivable. I'll have to have it towed back if it's not."

"Do you have triple A?"

"Yes, but here in Canada we call it CAA."

"When I went to get your suitcase, it looked okay. I think the snow softened the blow, but the air bag has been deployed, so you'll definitely need to call for a ride."

She turns toward her suitcase, the contents spilling out. She laughs. "I guess I was in kind of a hurry to get that off the bed last night."

"Just a bit, I'd say."

She breaks from my arms, and squats down next to her bag and starts folding her summer clothes. As I take in the disappointment on her face, it once again reminds me of what I was going to suggest to Trev yesterday when we were talking about his honeymoon.

She reaches for the pages that look like a play or something. "What's that?" I ask.

Her lips thin and for a second I don't think she's going to tell me. She flips through the pages. "It's a play I wrote with a classmate. Our class will be performing it at the end of the semester."

What the fuck?

"You wrote a play and your class is performing it?"

She shrugs, but her lips are twitching. "I love to act and write."

"I'm impressed."

She sets the papers down. "I'm supposed to be practicing. I was going to read and memorize my lines while lounging at the pool."

"You mean in between losing your virginity to some random guy?"

She laughs. "Something like that." She toys with the staple holding it together. "If I don't have this nailed by next month, Marcus is going to kill me."

"Marcus?" I say far too quickly. Jesus, I sound like a jealous boyfriend.

She doesn't pick up on that weird streak of possessiveness. Or if she did, she's not letting on or calling me out, which is a good thing. I don't want her to think I'm suddenly in love with her or something foolish like that.

"A fellow student. We wrote it together." She grins. "It's a love story, two kids who come from different backgrounds and have very little in common. Despite it all, they overcome the obstacles and profess their love."

"I'd love to read it."

"Come on, Chase. It's a romance. I can't imagine you read romance."

"Wow, judgy much?" I eye her. I guess it's a good thing I never told her I was a hockey player. She would have straight up written me off and never let me share her room. "You think you know everything about me," I tease.

"I never claimed that."

"Maybe there are things you don't know."

She puts her hands on her hips. "Like what, that you're a closet romantic?"

"Maybe."

She eyes me and from the grin slowly tugging up her lips, I'm not sure I'm going to like what's going through her head. "Maybe you could help me run lines."

"I don't know the first thing about acting, Sawyer." Okay, maybe that's not entirely true. After our games, I have to play to the crowd and sometimes talk to the reporters. That is me acting, because I'm not a guy who likes to be the center of attention at all.

"All you'd have to do is read Marcus's lines. You don't have to put emotions into them or anything like that."

"Let me see."

She hands the script over and I read the first few pages. "I guess I could do that."

"Really?" I nod and she grins excitedly. "You're the best, thank you." She goes onto her knees and shuffles toward me. Her arms go around my waist and she gives me a big kiss.

"Jeez, if reading with you gets me a kiss, what would I have to agree to in order to get you naked and back in this bed?"

She looks up to the left like she's considering it. "Probably not a lot."

"Here I thought I was the easy one."

I slide my hands around her neck and bring her mouth back to mine. I could stay just like this, and kiss her for the rest of the day, but her stomach grumbles, a reminder that we didn't make it down to dinner last night. I snuck out when she was asleep and turned the generator off to save gas, but I should get out there and turn it back on.

"I want you again, babe. Believe me I do. But you're sore, so I want to give you some time."

She huffs out, "Great."

"What?"

"That means today is going to be like yesterday, hours and hours of foreplay with me waiting to get back in this bed with you."

"Aww, I'm sorry, baby. Was it hard?"

She puts her hand over my crotch and feels my dick. "Yeah, it was hard."

More voices sound in the hall, and I stand up, and pull her with me. "Let's get out there and see what's happening with the plows."

"Okay. Do you mind if I wear your sweats again?"

"Not at all." I make a quick trip to the bathroom and when I come back, she's dressed and waiting for me, and dammit it's weird how much I like that. "All set?" She nods, and we leave the room. She goes quiet as we walk down the hall. "Everything okay?"

"Let's see," she begins with a chuckle. "I crashed my car, got saved by a hot guy, ended up sharing a room with him, and going on a snowmobile ride to get gas. Then we built a snowman, had a bonfire and skated. How do you think everything's going?"

"You think I'm hot?" I tease. She whacks me and we both laugh. "I think you're hot too."

She glances up at me, like she's not one hundred percent sure she believes that.

"Can I ask you something?" she asks.

"Yeah."

She casts me a fast glance. "What program interested you at the academy?"

For a split second I debate not telling her, but I don't think she'd laugh or shoot down the idea like my parents. "I had this buddy growing up. He lived on a farm, and I absolutely loved it there. He had horses, and goats, and cows. It was a lot of work taking care of the animals, but I just really loved it and the wide-open spaces."

She slows her steps and eyes me for a second. "You're talking about animal science, aren't you?"

I nod. "Is that strange?"

"No, I think it's awesome. What do you want to do with the degree?"

"I'm not even sure I'm going to do it, but I thought maybe down the road, I could do something in veterinary science."

"And have your own farm?"

"I'd really love that."

She laughs, but she's not laughing at me. "You know I can see that for you. Just look at how much Killer loved you. You have a way with animals."

"His name was Buster."

"We never had pets growing up. My mother always said she was allergic, but after she left..." Her voice falls off and I catch the sadness in her eyes as she glances away.

"I'm sorry, Sawyer. I didn't know."

We reach the stairs, and we go down them slowly, wanting to stretch out this private moment together.

"Yeah, I was just a kid."

That's why my comment on the sweater affected her. "That's hard." I capture her hand and give it a squeeze. I can't imagine what it was like for her growing up without a mother.

"I didn't have a father in my younger years. He passed away."

"Ohmigod, Chase. I'm so sorry."

Her look of mortification wraps around my heart. "My mom ended up marrying my dad's brother. He's a good guy, and I consider him my dad." She eyes me, like she can't quite wrap her brain around that, and I laugh. "It's a long story, and it sounds odd, I know. But it's a great story of love and triumph, and don't worry. I don't have daddy issues or anything." My only issue is my folks can't understand why I'd want to move to Canada. Hell, I'll still be in hockey, but I want a life when that's over and I want to carve my own path. "Do you...see your mom?"

"No, she left with Dad's best friend, actually. She's out west and she can stay there for all I care."

My heart pinches. Those are strong words, but there's pain there. "Anyway, all I was going to say was that after she left, I asked for a pet, but as Dad was taking the place of both mom and dad and I was busy with school, curling and drama, it just wouldn't be fair to an animal."

"Well, someday if I have a big farm, you can come stay for as long as you like, and play with all the animals. You could even keep a pet there." She smiles and I'm not sure if I just developed a brain tumor or something but the image of us on a farm together flashes in my brain. I like the image. Very much. I nearly topple off the last step to the main lobby.

"Are you okay?" she asks and reaches for me.

"Hungry," I fib and rub my stomach. A few guests are sitting around the fire, and Betsy is at the counter on her phone. We wave to her, and I turn to one of the elderly gentlemen as he nods to me. I think he said his name was Jack.

"Any news on the plow?" I ask.

"Betsy is talking with Malcolm now. It looks like we could be stuck here for another day or two."

"Two days, huh?" I sigh, like the idea of staying here is a real inconvenience, and he shakes his head in agreement.

"Two days too long, as far as I'm concerned," another man says, with a huff.

"You weren't in a hurry to get to my sister's place anyway, Harold," his wife Anna says and hits him with her small purse.

Harold winks at me over the newspaper that he's been reading for a couple of days. "True, but I'm missing my hockey."

"Aren't we all," someone else says.

"Not me," Sawyer mumbles under her breath. One of these days I'm going to have to find out what she has against the sport.

"Did you eat?" I ask.

"Yup, Danielle made us a feast."

"Good, we're going to grab something now."

We head down the hall to the café, where we find other guests still eating. That's when it occurs to me the lights are on. I didn't even bother checking in our room. We push through the swinging café doors that lead to the kitchen and find Danielle and Trev at the stove.

"Good morning," Danielle greets us, a big smile on her face. "I take it you both slept well." She has a knowing look on her face that says she's well aware of what we were up to last night and how could she not know when the walls are paper thin.

"We slept good." I turn to Trev who is popping toast, as Sawyer rushes in to help any way she can. "Thanks for getting the generator going."

"If we're here for a few more days," Trev says. "We might have to make another run to the gas station."

"We're going through gas fast, huh?"

"Yeah, that old generator is a beast." He hands me a plate. "Would you mind delivering?"

"No problem."

For the next twenty minutes, Danielle and Trev cook, and Sawyer and I deliver. Once everyone is fed and sitting back enjoying a cup of coffee, which I'm desperate for, I finally fill four cups and hand them around. We all take a moment to sip, before we help Danielle and Trev cook breakfast for the four of us. I nudge Trev, and keep my voice low, for his ears only.

"What are you guys doing tonight?" I have to save my plan for tonight, when the others have returned to their rooms. I guess I'm glad we're stranded with older couples who go to bed early. We're going to need an empty lobby for what I have planned.

He laughs. "Well, there's so much to do, we haven't been able to narrow down our choices yet."

I grin. "I have an idea."

He takes a sip of coffee and lowers his voice to match mine. "Am I going to like this idea?"

"Yeah, and the girls are going to love it."

"Then I'm in."

SAWYER

With sleep pulling at me, I flick off my flashlight and put down my script, my eyes and brain fading as I begin to drift off. A loud noise reverberates through me. I gulp, sit up, and glance around the dark room. My room is quiet, not a mouse stirring. Well, there are probably a lot of mice stirring, and I hope I don't see one. But by the sounds of things over head in the attic, I'd say we have more than mice stirring. There's so much banging around up there, I'm thinking it's a racoon or worse...

It's not a ghost, Sawyer.

As I work to settle my nerves—I am never going into that attic again—I flick on my flashlight, and walk to my window. I wipe the condensation and glance out into the dark night. Where the heck is Chase? After we had dinner, we all sat downstairs by the fire, and once everyone else went to bed, he and Trev said they had to go work on the generator. That was ages ago, and the generator has been off for about twenty minutes now. What's taking them so long? Shouldn't they be back? Then again, what do I know about generators? Nothing. All I can say is I'm glad the motel is still warm. Since it cools quickly however, maybe Chase and I can find creative ways to warm each other up.

I snatch my flashlight off the bed, and flick the light over the backyard, but Chase is nowhere to be found. Come to think of it, he was acting a bit strange tonight, almost antsy and anxious about something. I sigh heavily, knowing the reason why but not wanting to admit it. I'm not naïve enough to think he'd rather be here than with his friend. There are good times to be had in Halifax where he's not stuck in a motel, in bed with the only girl around his age. When he was chatting with Jack and Harold earlier, he made it sound like he was looking forward to seeing the plow and leaving this place behind.

I try to push that unwanted thought back as I walk back from the window and plunk back down on the bed. Maybe he doesn't plan to come back to our room tonight—I guess I'll never end up wearing that lingerie for him. Perhaps he's simply done with me. I know all about people walking away when they are done. Just as my worries peak, the door creaks open and I shine my flashlight toward it.

"Chase," I squeak, and jump up. He looks like he's trying to bite back a smile. "What's going on?"

"Hey," he whispers quietly, as he steps up to me, rubbing his hands up and down my arms, even though the place is still warm. "I was just hanging with Trev."

"Oh."

His gaze moves over my face. "Are you okay?"

"Yeah, it was late, and I was just worried about you. I wasn't sure what was going on." I yawn. "I'm just tired. My mind goes crazy when I'm tired."

"Thought you heard a ghost again?"

I point overhead. "You wouldn't believe the noises coming from up there. I think it was a sasquatch."

He laughs. "Nope, he's running around the woods in Seattle, not here."

I chuckle slightly as he gazes at me, and the mention that he's originally from Seattle reminds me we live different lives. "Do you want to go down and sit by the fire for a bit?"

"Oh, sure." I guess he's not quite ready for bed yet. I'm dressed in my jeans and a big sweater I found in the attic, and don't see a need to change into anything else. "Sounds cozy."

"Great." We walk to the door, and he stops.

"Hang on a second, okay?" He flicks on his flashlight and I wait as he walks into the room. I turn my light off to save the battery, and frown when I hear rustling sounds. He must be looking for something in his bag.

A second later, he's back at the door and he puts his fingers to his lips to hush me. As we step into the hall, walking quietly down the corridor, Danielle and Trev's door opens and Chase and Trev make eye contact. What the heck are they up to?

"Hey," Danielle whispers, sounding sleepy. "Are you guys coming to sit by the fire?"

"Yeah," I murmur, as Chase shines his light to illuminate the hallway. I loved the way he reaches behind him to hold my hand. As his big warm palm closes over mine, my heart thumps just a little too fast.

"Careful," he whispers when we reach the stairs. I grab the rail, my other hand still in his as we all form a straight line and make our way to the lobby in the dark. I can't see much since Chase is in front of me, his height and width blocking my view, but I think it will be really nice, and maybe romantic sitting in front of the fire.

After we all reach the landing, he turns to me, and the glow of the fire lights up his smiling face. Why is he grinning like that?

"Okay," he begins. "It's not Florida." His gaze goes to Danielle as Trev stands in front of her, blocking her view too.

"And it's not Jamaica," Trev says to Danielle as he takes both of her hands in his.

"Okay," I say trying to see around Chase's broad body.

Chase squeezes my hand and looks like he's about to burst. "But under the circumstances, it's the best we could do."

"Working with what we had," Trev adds. They both step to the side, and I gasp when I see all the candles, a table with different kinds of liquor, and a children's plastic swimming pool in front of the fire. The water inside glistens in the flickering flames.

"What did you do?" I practically shriek.

"Shh." Chase puts his finger to his lips. Beside me, Danielle laughs, and goes up on her toes to kiss her husband.

"We brought the beach to you, sort of," Chase explains with a laugh. "Trev and I will be your pool boys." He takes my hand, and puts something soft in it. I glance down to find my bikini.

"This is what you ran back for?" Shock and pleasure race through me.

"Yes," he says, going from one foot to the other, like an excited kid on Christmas morning. It's a wonder he could keep the secret this long. "Surprise," he whispers, and presses his lips to mine. I kiss him deeply, my heart somewhere in my throat. I can't believe this is what he and Trevor were up to.

"You're full of surprises," I tell him as I lean into him, his big hands circling my body and holding me tight.

"You like it?"

"I love it."

"Good, now go in the bathroom, get into your bikini, and get in the water before it turns cold."

"Come on," Danielle squeals just as excited as I am. She turns on her flashlight and we both dart into the bathroom, and strip off our heavy clothes.

"Can you believe this?" I say, still trying to wrap my brain around it. No one has ever done anything like this for me before.

"Trev says it was Chase's idea." She grins at me, and my butterflies erupt in my stomach. "He's kind of sweet."

"He is," I admit, and try not to smile like the village idiot. I fail, of course, but in the dark, Danielle can't see me.

"Fate is a funny thing, isn't it?" she says.

"Meaning?"

"You two never would have met if there was no snowstorm."

I nod, but again, she can't see me. Would we have met? Maybe our paths were meant to cross in Halifax. If he decides to switch colleges, we'd be on the same campus. Although animal science and the department aren't even near each other. Still, Halifax has numerous pubs, and everyone seems to know everyone, so it could have happened. Then again, he's pretty damn hot, and maybe he wouldn't have given me the time of day once there were other girls in the picture, I have no doubt he'd have his pick at the academy. He said it's been a long time since he's been with anyone. Maybe that's not true. Although I can't see why he'd lie to me about that and I don't want to think badly of him. So, I won't. Instead, I shut down those thoughts, tug on my bikini bottoms, and tie my top around my neck.

"Do you think you guys will continue to see each other after we're plowed out?"

See each other?

My heart sinks a little. I'm not even sure I should entertain that thought. What we're doing here is having sex. There's not more going on between us, right? Heck, a relationship could jump up and smack me in the face and I wouldn't even know it. I've never been in anything long term, or short term for that matter, and what if I give consideration to us, only to realize that what we're really doing here is just sex—a means to entertain ourselves during the white out?

"I'm not really sure."

Danielle threads her arm through mine. "I think you two make a cute couple."

"Thanks," I say as my throat squeezes tight. Goddammit, I wasn't supposed to let my emotions get involved. Honestly though, how could I not when he goes out of his way and plans something like this? I can see Trev doing it. He's married to Danielle.

But it was Chase's idea.

I glance around the room and chuckle when I see Chase and Trev standing there, towels over their arms as they pretend to be pool boys. Would a guy who's just interested in sex do something like this? If it was a means to an end—his way to get sex—then the answer could be yes.

We walk up to the pool and I dip my toes in. "Aren't you guys getting in?"

Chase laughs. "I'm afraid I'd displace all that water, and you'd be sitting on nothing but plastic." I take that moment to look at his body, blatantly eyeing him up and down, and like everything I see.

"Okay ladies, would you like a cocktail? A pina colada, perhaps."

"Oh, sounds good," Danielle says, and I debate on whether to have one or not. When I had wine, Chase didn't want to have sex, didn't want to take advantage of the situation, but I think we're in a different position now. Speaking of positions...I envision all the things he still has to teach me as I meet his gaze, and he grins at me, like he can read my dirty thoughts.

"I think that sounds just about right, too." I step into the warm water and sink down. The fire flickers over the room and I push all worries aside. I exhale, a new kind of contentment coming over me, as I pretend the fire is the sun warming my body.

"Here you go." I open my eyes as Chase drops to the floor beside the pool and hands me a drink.

I take a big mouthful and moan in pleasure. "Where did you get this?"

"Café..." he leans in and whispers. "Please don't moan like that."

I laugh at his silliness, and he dips his hand into the water and splashes it over my chest. Thank God it's warm.

"Who's ready for a snack?"

"I am," Danielle answers. "Is the pool boy going to feed me grapes?" Foil crinkles and I turn to Trev as he opens a bag of potato chips. He pops one into his mouth and crunches it.

"There were no grapes. Will chips do?" Danielle opens her mouth, and he pops a chip in.

Chase produces a bag and hold it up to see if I want it. "Yes please." Heat passes over his eyes. Was it something I said? Maybe I'll have to remember that for later, because yeah, there's definitely going to be a later. Trev tosses Chase a can of beer and he cracks it and takes a big drink.

Trev jumps up and turns on the old radio behind the counter, and it starts playing all those old songs Betsy loves. "I tried to find another channel, but I don't think the twenty-first century has reached this part of Nova Scotia yet." I laugh at that, and cover my mouth to quiet myself.

"You could always serenade us," Danielle suggests.

"Hell no," Chase bursts out. "No one wants to hear me sing."

"Okay, now I really do," I say.

"You're the performer, not me."

I reach out and touch his face. "It's okay. I'd never want you to do anything that would make you embarrassed."

"Whew," he gasps in relief, and wipes his brow.

I chuckle, and lean back into the small pool, wanting to enjoy every moment of this. Conversation turns to Danielle and Trev, and they tell us how they met, and talk about their wedding. I sit in wonderment. I was never a girly girl who dreamed about her wedding. In fact, I was pretty sure I was never going to meet Mr. Right. I turn to Chase, who is listening closely to our new friends. Is he the kind of guy who thinks about marriage and kids? He said he'd like to own a farm someday. Does that farm include a family? I'm not sure, and while I am curious, the future is for the future and tonight is for tonight.

I dip my hand into the cooling water and splash him. He jerks back. "Hey."

"Oh no, it looks like you're all wet." I nibble on my bottom lip, and he angles his head, no doubt wondering what I'm up to. "I guess we should head upstairs and get you out of those wet clothes, huh? We wouldn't want you to catch a cold."

He grins and as he stands and holds his hand out to help me up, I know I'm in far too deep, and it's obvious I'm not talking about the water in the shallow kiddie pool.

15

CHASE

As I help Sawyer from the small pool, Trev hops in, taking her place, which makes us all laugh. My chuckle comes out rough and husky—compliments of my arousal—as I wrap a big towel around Sawyer's petite body, and pull her into the circle of my arms to keep her warm. A fine shiver goes through her and vibrates all the way to my balls, as I rub her arms to keep her warm.

"I agree we'd better get upstairs and out of these wet clothes," I tell the newlyweds, trying my best to sound normal, when my heart is beating so hard it's making me breathless and...twitchy. What the hell is going on with me? I've been with numerous women, and have never acted like a green boy with his first boner. Fuck, all I know is how much I like the girl in my arms, and how much I hate the idea of not seeing her again after we're plowed out. I've never felt so close to anyone before. There's an undeniable intimacy in everything we do, inside the bedroom and out. Perhaps it's just the romance and ambience created by being forced together during a storm...or perhaps it's something else. Does she feel it too? I'd like to ask, but if she doesn't, I could very well scare her off. Maybe I'm making more out of this than there really is.

"Night guys," Danielle says as I gather up Sawyer's clothes, wave to our new friends who are cozy and warm in front of the fire, and use my flashlight to guide us to the stairs.

"See you in the morning," Sawyer says, her voice low, thick with arousal as she gives a little finger wave.

I keep her tucked in tight next to me as we climb the staircase and head down the long, quiet hall. There's a different kind of energy between us tonight, a warmth that goes right to my core and tugs at something deep. I open the door to our room and usher her in, locking it behind us. I don't want any interruptions, even though I'm sure everyone is fast asleep. She leaves my arms, goes to the dresser and grabs something.

She flicks on her flashlight. "I'm just going to go to the bathroom to get changed."

"Um...I've seen you naked," I remind her, and she gives an almost nervous, edgy chuckle as I tug off my sweater and rip into my pants, my cock aching to be inside her again.

"I'll just be a second."

Having no idea what she's up to or what she has hidden behind her back as she darts to the bathroom, I pull the blankets down, fluff up the pillows, climb in and roll to my side as I wait for her. A few minutes pass and I begin to worry.

"You okay in there?"

Was that a bang?

I'm about to get up and check on things when the bathroom door creeps open. I shine my light on her, and my heart tumbles in my chest as she comes out wearing a red, one-piece silky number that I hadn't seen in her suitcase earlier. If I had I would have remembered it. It leaves little to the imagination and on anyone else it would be sexy. Wait, that's not coming out right. It's not that it's not sexy on her, it is, but the best word to describe it is...I don't know. I really don't know. All I know is that everything about this, about her is perfect and she's the most beautiful girl I've ever set eyes on.

How did I get so fucking lucky?

"Did you...put that on for me?" Christ, I can barely talk. Looking at her is choking me up, and that's never happened before. Did she have it tucked away somewhere secret, with the plans to wear it for some random guy in Florida.

"Do you like it?" She walks to the bottom of the bed and sways.

"No."

"No?" she says, her big eyes going wide.

I crook my finger and gesture her close. "I love it." She laughs and the sound cradles my heart. "But I want it off you."

She puts one hand on her hip. "No, you're going to sit there and look at me in it." I angle my head and try to figure out what is going on. "It took me forever to get into this." She points to her crotch. "It has snaps down there. I thought I was going to put my neck out trying to get it fastened."

This time I'm the one laughing. Could she be any sweeter? Her honesty really fucks me over. "Why would you buy something like that if you were going to hurt yourself putting it on?"

"I didn't buy it." She looks almost sheepish as she adds, "Danielle was given this as a gift, she thought it would look better on me than her. I just didn't know I'd have to be a contortionist to get into it."

"She was right, it does look better on you."

"Really now. Are you saying you saw it on her?"

"Nope, and I don't want to." It's the truth. The only one I want to see in lingerie is Sawyer. "I just know these things." I gesture with a nod. "Now get over here so I can see you better."

I keep the light on her as she steps toward me, an extra sway to her hips that brings a big smile to her face. I like when she's being playful and seductive, and while she doesn't need to do that, or to wear special clothes, I appreciate the effort. So does my dick. He's currently standing up, working to get a better look at the gorgeous girl sauntering our way.

I put my feet on the floor as she stops at the side of the bed, and I press my nose to her chest, breathing her in as my hands move up her sides, the silky material soft to my fingertips. But I want it gone. Her body is that much softer—a welcome contrast to the hardness of mine.

I put my finger between her legs and slide them across the warm snaps, although I'm not ready to undress her, not after she put so much effort into getting into the outfit. Her hips slant forward as I lightly stroke her and I put my mouth on her nipple, kissing her through the fabric. Her back arches, her hands going around my neck, holding me to her, and I love that she's comfortable enough with me to show me what she likes. She moans and I pull back, taking her other nipple into my mouth.

"So good," she murmurs.

I glance at the two wet spots on the material, and for some reason it makes my cock even harder.

"I've missed these."

"They were always here," she murmurs playfully. I take my hands out from between her legs, cup both her breasts and squeeze gently, lifting her cleavage until her soft skin is plump and visible. I kiss her creamy flesh and tug the material downward until I have her nipples exposed, mine for the taking. I lick and suck them until she's moaning and my cock is screaming, and while I'd like to push my cock between her breasts and fuck her, I have to get my mouth between her legs first.

I slide my fingers back between her hot thighs, and she widens her legs for me. The flashlight grows dim, but the moonlight shining in falls over her body and I take her in, loving the way her chest rises and falls with need, her eyes barely open as I touch her. She loves me touching her as much as I love touching her, and tonight, we're going to do so many things. She wants to learn, and I want to teach.

That thought suddenly tastes sour in my mouth. She came to me a virgin with questions, and when she leaves here she'll have new experiences—that she'll be able to use other guys. Fuck me.

"Chase," she murmurs as the sound of the first snap opening fills the silence surrounding us. "Please..."

I chuckle. "Please what?"

"Please touch me."

"You need my hands on you, Sawyer?" It's crazy how much I want to hear her say it.

"I do. It's been one long day of torturously delicious foreplay."

"Don't I know it. You in that bikini, and then in this hot number. It's a wonder it hasn't fried all my brains cells." She smiles, liking that. Her hands rake through my hair and she kisses me as I release the second snap, freeing the material keeping me away from her hot pussy, which I can't seem to get enough of.

I slide my finger over her wet lips, and it makes me happy to know she's excited. "Mmm," I moan as my mouth waters. She moves her body, sliding her cunt over my finger.

"More," she begs, and wiggles trying to force my finger inside and I can't hold out any longer, not when we're both so desperate for it.

"You like my finger in here?" I ask as I slide into her, and her head rolls to the side, her hair tumbling over her shoulder.

"It feels so good, Chase."

"You feel good," I tell her as I go still again, encouraging her to fuck my finger. She catches on quickly and I sit on the edge of the bed, my finger in her as she energetically rides my finger. Her sounds of pleasure, her moans, the way her pussy muscles are lightly clenching around my finger already...let's just say it's the hottest, most goddamn beautiful thing I've ever had the pleasure of viewing. I put another finger in her for a snugger fit and she begins to move faster, her body chasing an orgasm.

Helping her out, I lean into her and circle her clit with my tongue. "You are so good at that," She whimpers as I eat at her and let her fuck my fingers. Her body tightens even more and I stand up, my fingers still inside her.

"Chase," she moans, not knowing what she's supposed to do. I don't want her doing anything but enjoying this, and I need to get her off her shaky legs. I turn her, never removing my fingers and sit her on the bed. She goes back on her hands, opening her body to me, and I drop to my knees and bury my face in her sweet cunt.

"I...love...this..." she gasps, taking deep gulping breaths as I pump into her, and slide my tongue over her swollen, achy clit. "Everything you do...so good."

My cock is raging, aching to plunge into her but I have other plans for tonight, plans that I think she'll like for numerous reasons. "Still want to learn new things?"

"Yes..." she cries out, her body tightening, preparing for the onslaught of pleasure my fingers and mouth are about to wring out of her.

Her head goes from side to side and she cups her breasts. I nearly lose my load as she squeezes those gorgeous tits, providing the perfect channel for me to fuck.

"Don't stop, please don't stop."

"I won't stop," I assure her as I bring every nerve ending to life.

Her lids pinch shut, and my name crawls out of her throat, a high-pitched cry as pleasure centers in her core and she bursts around my fingers.

"Fuck yeah," I say, and lick her, lapping up her hot juices as she moans and squeezes my fingers harder. "Look at you, coming all over my fingers again."

She goes up on her elbows, her breathing erratic and her face flushed as I keep my fingers inside her, wringing, and drawing out the last of her orgasm. Fuck, I could get used to doing this to her.

"Chase," she chants as her body begins to settle, and I take my fingers from her pussy, and smile at her. She smiles back, her eyes soft and glossy. I spread my legs, climb over her and move her to the middle of the bed. My cock juts out, inches from her face as I reposition. She opens her mouth, ready to take me in, but I have other ideas. I shimmy back and her brow scrunches together.

I squeeze her breasts and nearly drool on them. She eyes my cock as pre-come drips from the slit. "I want to taste you."

"You will," I say and it's a promise I made to her before and tonight plan to keep. "Put your hands where mine are."

She does and I remove mine, positioning my cock over her creamy skin. My come drips and I rub it between her breasts for lubrication.

"Oh, God," she murmurs her body quaking as she figures out what I'm about to do. "No guy has ever fucked you like this, right?" I already know the answer. There's just a part of me that wants to hear her say it.

"No."

"Good." I slide my dick between her slicked-up breasts and pump forward, coming close to her face. "Open your mouth."

She widens her lips and her tongue looks so wet, a gloriously soft landing pad. My cock jumps, eager to spill on that sweet tongue. Her eyes move to my cock as I turn my entire focus to it, desperate to appease the need pummeling my body and battering my brain. I rock into her tits, and she squeezes them around me.

"Fuck, Sawyer." I grunt, having no idea how I'm going to go more than a few good thrusts. I want her too much, and I'm not even sure math is going to help me hold back. The need pulling at me is insane, too much for me to handle as pleasure sharpens in my balls.

"Mmm," she murmurs, her tongue still out like a girl doing exactly what I told her to do—and exactly what she wants. It's fucking mind-blowing how much she wants my cock and my cum. I push a little deeper, my crown spilling droplets of pre-cum on her tongue and watching it drop from the soft blade to her chest is more than any man in his right mind—or wrong mind—can take.

"I am not going to last," I grunt through gritted teeth.

She doesn't say anything. Instead she just lays there, tongue out, waiting for me to come in her mouth. "Sawyer..." I pump once, then twice and shove my cock into her mouth as a powerful orgasm slams into me. I spurt into her mouth, and she lifts herself up, stretching her lips around my swollen crown. She gobbles up my cum, and drinks me in and it's fucking beautiful. She licks and sucks and cleans me up, and I can't seem to do anything but breathe as I watch her. Once she's done, she lays back on the pillow and I pull my cock out.

"That's exactly what I wanted," she whispers. I shift my body until I'm beside her and cup her face and shake my head in sheer bewilderment. Who the hell is this woman, and what is she doing to me?

She moans in contentment, and I say, "It was perfect."

"Yeah," she murmurs in agreement, looking spent and sated and so goddamn pleasured my throat squeezes tight. I did this to her. I'm the guy she trusted with her body, and because of that she did the most amazing things to mine. Honestly, I'm not so sure I'm deserving, especially after keeping who I really am from her. If I tell her now, will she hate me, never want to see me again. Probably. But was there ever a chance that we could have something when we left here? Even if there was, I probably fucked that all up by not coming right out and telling her who I am, and why I'm really headed to Halifax.

Well fucking done, Chase.

16

SAWYER

I stand on the ice and shake my head as Chase throws his rock, and knocks mine off its mark. We're not playing a real game of curling here—I only had two rocks in the car—but his aim is perfect. I wish I had my broom so I could sweep his rock and control the direction it moves.

He turns to me, throws his hands in the air, and gloats, "I have no equal." I laugh and fake punch him in the stomach. He grunts and bends forward.

"Do you have to be good at everything you do?" I ask.

"What can I say—"

"You have no equal. Right, I got it."

I glance over at Danielle and Trev, who are warming themselves around the fire, and I take a big breath, contentment moving through my body as the late day sun shines down on me. I'm sure the plow trucks are going to be here any time now and I have to say, I'm not ready to leave.

"Want to throw them a couple more times?" Chase asks, pulling my thoughts back.

"Do you really like it?" He walks to get our rocks. "I mean, you're American."

"What does 'you're American mean'?" He turns and grins at me, and my pulse leaps as he presents me with that cute dimple.

"Don't all Americans think curling is ridiculous, and that it's not even a sport?"

"I can't speak for all Americans, but I think it's kind of fun. Maybe I'll join a team." I laugh, and he says, "You're pretty good at this. I can see why your father wanted you to go professional, but you have to do what you love and if this isn't it…"

I throw my hands up. "Parents." He glances at the ice, and his shoulders sag a bit. "Speaking of doing what we want and love, yours don't like the idea of animal science, huh?"

He laughs, but it holds no humor. "No, they don't really understand it."

I want to ask him what his parents do for a living, but then that could lead to a discussion on my dad and I don't want to talk about hockey. He doesn't need to know how the players treat me, or how they make horrible bets. Honestly, it's embarrassing, and I just want to bury all those memories and enjoy what little time we have left here. Besides, if he wanted me to know more about him, he'd tell me, which is a little niggling reminder that we're not opening up fully or sharing more of ourselves than necessary. When we're gone from here, what's happening between us stays here.

"Who wants a marshmallow?" Danielle calls out.

"Me," I shout back, needing a distraction before I go deeper down that rabbit hole. Who am I kidding? I'm in so deep with Chase now, I'm not sure I'll ever be able to dig myself out.

Why did you let your stupid heart get involved, Sawyer?

Oh, because he's so goddamn sweet and thoughtful, it was impossible not to. I'm about to leave, when Chase puts his arm around me, and drags me to his body. He spins me around, and a puff of breath fills the air as I gasp and laugh.

"What are you doing?" I ask, and instead of answering, his lips find mine for a deep, sensuous kiss. I put my arms around his neck, uncaring that Danielle and Trev are watching, and for one long minute I forget that I have no future with this guy despite the fact that I want one. He breaks the kiss and I smile up at him.

"I didn't know you were into public displays of affection."

"I'm not. You're the actress not me. I like to stay in the shadows. I just couldn't help myself."

"I think you'd be a great actor."

"You're just saying that so I'll run lines with you tonight."

I crinkle my nose, and pretend to be offended. "Is that what you think of me?"

"Is it true."

"Well..."

He laughs. "That's what I thought."

"Does this mean you'll do it?"

"Yeah, sure. As long as we don't have an audience. I'm looking forward to reading your play. Wait, I'll be reading the hero's part, right?"

"Yes, but..." I nibble my lips. "I'm not your leading lady."

"What the hell? You wrote it."

"I know but there were auditions at school, and..." Ugh. "I'm never the leading lady." I'm just never good enough and I'm always overlooked. But I don't tell him that.

"That's ridiculous. Give me five minutes with your instructors and I'll straighten them out."

"Ooh, tough guy," I tease simply to hide my embarrassment. I did write the play and I should be the lead. I sigh inwardly, and hate to admit it, but I think there's a part of me that knows I'm not good enough. I wasn't enough my mother, that's for sure.

With his arm around me, we both go silent, lost in our thoughts as we walk to the bonfire and plunk down on the log. A rumbling noise, far in the distant reaches my ears and I sit up a little straighter.

"Do you guys hear that?"

"It must be the plow," Trev says and jumps from the log. He glances in the distance, but there's only a bed of white all around us.

Danielle stands on the log and looks around. "Maybe we should head inside and see if there's news from Malcolm."

I sit there, unmoving, and don't want to appear upset that we're getting plowed out. That would give Chase the wrong signals, or rather the right ones. Ignoring the knot in my stomach I jump up. "About time. But I guess that's to be expected here in Folly Mountain." I turn to Chase. "Told you it'd be days."

"You weren't wrong." Chase says and stands up next to me.

"Hopefully you can still get some fun activities in with your friend."

"Yeah," is all he says as he walks away and goes to the ice to get my rocks. He carries both of them like they don't weigh forty-four pounds each.

We all trek back to the motel, and there's old time music blaring in the main lobby when we enter. A smile stretches across my face as the guests are all dancing to some ancient song that I don't recognize.

Trev laughs. "Looks like there's a party going on and they forgot to invite us."

"Rude," I joke.

Danielle's face lights up. "I guess they must be celebrating because they heard good news."

I wave to Betsy who comes dancing over. "What's going on?"

"Malcolm called." She claps her hands to her rosy cheeks. "They brought in equipment from the city. We should be all plowed out by tomorrow at the latest." My heart sinks a little deeper into my chest. "Isn't that great news?"

"The best," I agree and put on my biggest happiest smile. I should win an Oscar for this performance, and yet my instructors never give me the lead.

"Although I must say, I have enjoyed having you all here." Her thin lips pinch together, and I sense her loneliness. "Things haven't been the same since I lost my Billy."

"I'm so sorry," I say, and give her hand a little squeeze.

"Is that the...tango?" Danielle asks, her head angled as she tries to figure out the music and the dance.

"Come tango with me," Betsy says and grabs hold of Chase. She jerks him forward. My God, she's much stronger than she looks.

"I don't know how," Chase blurts out.

"I'll teach you."

Chase casts me a pleading gaze and I shrug and laugh as Betsy whisks him into the fray. He stumbles a bit, which surprises me because he's a fast learner and he's good at everything he does. My body warms as I watch the two, and Danielle and Trev jump in and I watch the others to learn the steps. My heart misses a couple beats, loving everything about this.

"Get over here," Harold yells, and I hold my hands up and give a fast shake of my head, but he snatches one hand and pulls, refusing to let me remain an innocent bystander. I step on his feet a few times before I get the hang of it, and in no time at all, I'm dancing and loving it.

"Change partners," Betsy calls out and Harold lets me go. Chase snatches me up as Anna eyes him, and pulls my body to his.

"Nice moves, Sawyer."

"You're not so bad yourself, Chase," I chuckle, shaking my head and laughing with him. "I never thought I'd learn the tango on this vacation." Then again, I'm doing a lot of things, learning a lot of things I never thought I would. My plan was to rid myself of my pesky virginity. A wham bam thank you ma'am sort of deal. Falling for the hot guy who rescued me in so many ways, that was completely unexpected.

Catching me by surprise, Chase spins me, and I shriek when he nearly loses his grip. He tugs me back, and I collide with his hard body.

"I thought I was going to faceplant," I tell him.

"I've got you."

"I know. I'm in good hands," I say, and my body warms, remembering the last time I told him that, and what followed. The song ends, and I'm breathless but it's not from exertion. "That was fun." Everything I do with Chase is fun.

"Dinner is served," someone announces, banging a ladle on a pot as they come into the main lobby. I turn to see Carol and laugh when I see how light it still is outside. "Is it even five yet?"

"Early bird special," I say, and Danielle leans into me.

"A night off cooking on my honeymoon. I'll take the early bird special." Betsy goes and turns the music down and my stomach grumbles as we reach the café. I guess I built up an appetite teaching Chase how to curl, along with the dancing, and who am I to complain that it's too early to eat. I'm starving.

"Tonight's special is shepherd's pie," Carol says. "Good and hearty, a stick to the ribs comfort meal." She smiles at Danielle. "I wanted to give you a break."

"You're sweet, and thank you."

We all make our way to the tables, and Chase and I sit with our friends. As I glance at them, I can't help but think how nice it would be if the four of us double-dated at some point in the future, but then I remember Chase and I don't have a future. I stare at the plate of food placed in front of me, my appetite dwindling.

"You don't like it?" Chase asks.

"Oh, no I love it. I was just thinking about my car and calling CAA," I say, and grab my fork and dig in. It's a fib but now is not the right time to tell him what I'm really thinking...what I'm really feeling. Is there a right time though? What if I did tell him? What if I let him know that I'd like to continue with what we're doing when we're all plowed out? Am I being silly? He doesn't even know if he's going to stay in Nova Scotia.

Give him a reason to stay?

As that thought jumps into my brain, I turn to find Chase smiling at me. "What?" I ask.

"So messy." He tucks a strand of hair behind my ear, his fingers lightly grazing my cheek and my heart goes haywire.

"I'm not messy."

"Tell that to the corn on your face."

I swipe at my face and a piece of corn goes flying across the table. Everyone laughs, myself included. "Okay, maybe I am messy, but you're messy too."

"I am not," he says, and I flick a piece of corn at him. It lands in his hair, and he swats at it. "Jesus girl, you're going to pay for that."

"Come at me, bro," I joke, and he laughs harder.

"You're right. I shouldn't challenge a girl who can swing forty-four-pound rocks."

"I think you mean nineteen-point-one kilograms." I nudge him.

"Canadians," he says, laughing, but it does remind me we're different people from different worlds, different countries even. It never seemed to matter while we were stuck here. Will it matter when we're not?

"Tell me more about curling," Danielle says. "It really looked like you two were having fun." She nudges Trev. "Maybe we could take up the sport. We could get really good, and play against Sawyer and Chase."

"How about we play doubles," Trev suggests. "They were both good and I want them on my team."

"I want Sawyer on my team, for sure," Chase says and as they all talk about curling, I shift a little closer to the man I'm falling for, loving the comradery between the four of us. I smile up at him, as he puts his arm around me, insisting he be on my team. I can't help but think we do make a good team in a lot of ways and I don't want this to end.

So, what are you going to do about that, Sawyer?

"I can't believe you wrote this." Sawyer arches her brow, all playfully indignant, and I continue with, "I don't mean I'm surprised by your talent or anything. It's just wow. It's so good. Look out Hollywood."

She laughs and smacks me with the script pages in her hand. "While that's very nice of you to say, I don't have my sights set on Hollywood or anything like that."

"What do you want to do?" I ask as we leave our room and head downstairs to the main lobby, where I'm going to help her run lines.

"I want to act, and maybe open my own little theater somewhere around here. I love Nova Scotia—"

"Yeah, from April to November."

"Okay, I did say that, but this December was kind of fun. I guess I just forgot that the snow can be fun too."

"Tell me about this theater."

She smiles, and I get the sense she likes when I take an interest in her things, but I really do want to know everything about her.

"I want to stay here and nurture the talent in our area. We have so much talent. There are also great incentives for filming here, and the industry is booming. I don't need or want to go anywhere else."

"That all sounds amazing. Do you have a specific spot in mind for your theater?"

"Not yet, but..." Her eyes open, a new animation about her as she talks about her love of theater. I really love that she's found her passion and is pursuing it. "There was this place in Chester, called Chester's Playhouse. I used to go there all the time, but it burnt down a couple of years ago. I would love to build something like that. Hire locals for plays."

"So, you could do that anywhere. You don't have to be in the city."

She shrugs. "Chester is a small community on the outskirts of Halifax. About a thirty-minute drive. If a playhouse can thrive there, it can thrive anywhere. Nova Scotia is very supportive of the arts, and it's a culturally rich province."

I nod as I consider that. "I'd come see you."

She smiles. "All the way from Boston?" She nudges me. "That's a pretty long return trip, Chase."

I just laugh, but I have to say, moving to Halifax and going to Scotia Academy is sounding better and better, and I haven't even checked out the curriculum or the team yet. But staying means that maybe we could continue seeing each other and build on what's blossoming between us. Would she like the idea of that?

"Maybe I'll fall in love with Halifax and the academy and stay," I say, shining my flashlight on her to see her reaction. "Then I wouldn't have that big-ass commute."

She nods. "Halifax is an easy place to fall in love with."

Sawyer is easy to fall in love with.

But if I stay, the truth about who I really am, and that I've been drafted will come out, and not only does she hate hockey players, she's not going to like that I kept that from her. Would she understand why I omitted that piece of myself? That I just wanted us to get to know one another without all the bullshit. That I liked being myself around her, no pressure, no expectations. No judgement, no pretense.

I nudge her. "Maybe you could show me around."

"I'd be happy to."

"And of course, I'd get a big discount on tickets at this playhouse you're going to run, right?"

"What makes you think I'd give you preferential treatment?"

"Uh, I did save your ass in a snowstorm."

She laughs loudly, then quickly covers her mouth. "I think I rescued you. You would have been driving these back roads lost for days on end if you didn't pick me up."

"Nice twist to the story, but true."

"I'm kidding. I'm really glad you saw me and stopped. I hate to think what might have happened if you didn't."

She frowns and glances down, like she's remembering something, and my mind goes back to our first conversation in the car, when I said I barely saw her. I get it now, but I don't get it. From what I've learned about her, it's clear she is used to being overlooked, and I honestly can't wrap my brain around that. She's gorgeous, fun and wildly talented. Why would anyone overlook her? I want to ask but I don't want to upset her.

She shines her light on the hallway as we quietly walk down it, and I consider her answer. Does that mean she wants me to stay? That I'm not the only one falling head over heels here?

We reach the bottom of the stairs and fire from the hearth lights up the room. I glance around, and the place is empty. Everyone has gone to bed already, no doubt dreaming about getting out of here tomorrow. Maybe the plow trucks won't make it and maybe we'll be here longer. And maybe that's just wishful thinking on my part.

I lift the script up and read over the lines I'm supposed to give. "I'm not going to be very good at this."

"You'll be fine. Just read. You don't have to put any emotions or action into it. It just helps me get my cues."

"I'm not an extrovert like you." I'm kind of envious of her ability to perform. Maybe I'd do a hell of a lot better in interviews if I wasn't always looking to escape back to obscurity.

"Okay," she begins. "So I'm the lead's best friend, and what's going on in this scene is you and me." She pokes her finger into my chest. "Not me, my character and yours are secretly in love. Neither one knows how the other feels...they're both afraid of voicing it."

My God, isn't that the story of my life right now. Then again, I know how I feel, but I'm not too sure about her.

"And you're telling me that Stefanie—that's the main character's name, and your girlfriend in the play—told you she was pregnant, and of course that's forcing you to stay with her."

"Complicated much?"

"What is a play without drama and conflict?"

"Uh, words on paper." Really, I have no idea. I'm not much of a reader, and English class was never my favorite.

She laughs. "Something like that. Are you ready?"

I glance around the room, fidgeting a bit. I am so not the guy who likes an audience and I actually feel weird with Sawyer watching me.

"I'll start," she says, and I stare at her as she recites her lines, adding emotions and action and for a brief second, I forget that she's acting, and not actually talking to me. She finishes and I stare at her for a second.

"This is where you read." She points to the name Caleb on the paper. "That's you."

"Yeah, okay." I clear my throat and put my hand over my heart. "It's true," I begin. "She's pregnant, and she wants to get married."

Sawyer takes a step closer to me, her body heat reaching out to me, wrapping around my body and squeezing tight. "But do you love her, Caleb? You can't..." She swallows hard, and chokes up a bit as she glances down. "You need to be with the one you love. Tell me she's the one you love."

I put my hand on her face, the way the script directs me, and her glossy eyes, full of hope and worry, lift to mine. Christ, she's good, and for a brief second I forget we're acting, and I'm about to tell her it's her I love. My gaze falls to the script, and I begin, "Stefanie, she's the one..." My sentence falls off, and I read the next line to discover that Stefanie is to enter the room and it's the end of the scene. I look up to find Sawyer smiling at me. "What?"

"I think maybe you're just kidding about not being an extrovert."

"Would I lie about something like that?" I flick the paper and read my next line, which is directed at Stefanie. Then Sawyer does an exchange with Caleb. We move to the next scene, and continue to recite the words on the page for a good fifteen minutes and Sawyer's barely looked at her script. I think she has the part nailed, although she should have the lead. I flip my page and we read some more, and then suddenly my words catch in my throat when the power bursts back on, all through the motel, flicking on the lights and furnace and everything else until there's a hum going through the old building.

My heart jumps, but it's not because we suddenly have power, it's because we have a big audience on the stairs.

"Oh God," I groan and put the script over my face.

"How long have you all been there?" Sawyer asks.

"About ten minutes," Danielle tells us.

Harold clears his throat. "Long enough to know we all want to see the rest of the play, to see how it all turns out."

"I am mortified," I groan and drop the papers to find them all staring. Trev starts clapping and I'm sure my face must be a hundred shades of red. Everyone joins in the clapping.

"Let's take a bow, my friend," Sawyer says, and stands beside me. She captures my hand and plays along. Even though I'm ridiculously embarrassed, I bend and wave my hand.

"Did you know they were there?" I ask Sawyer.

"No, I would never do that to you."

"Yeah, I know," I murmur. She's one of the few people who knows I don't like the spotlight—one of the few people I can really be myself around—and she's not the kind of girl to set me up for embarrassment.

"Sorry, bro," Trev apologizes. "Didn't mean to embarrass you. We all decided we'd have a night of charades. We tried your door but no answer, and we thought...." He grins. "Well, it doesn't matter what we thought."

Everyone comes into the room and claps us on the back. Conversation turns to Sawyer and her acting classes, the group more excited about her play than the fact that we now have electricity.

Sawyer animatedly tells them about the playhouse theater she someday wants to open and they all promise to visit.

Trev comes up to me and hands me a beer. "You're a natural thespian," he says.

"Far from it." I laugh and take a big swig of my beer.

Harold walks up to us. "Frank and I were trying to figure out why you looked so familiar. Now I guess we know. What have you acted in?"

"I'm not an actor." I shift from one foot to the other, uncomfortable under his scrutiny, not to mention the guilt flooding my veins.

He winks and nudges me with his elbow. "Ah, I see, you're going incognito, not wanting to cause a ruckus."

Ruckus?

"Don't worry your secret is safe with us," Harold promises.

"Okay, good." I play along because he's convinced he knows me.

As Harold walks away, I turn and note the way Trev is studying me, and I know the second recognition hits by the way his eyes widen.

Shit.

"Chase," he begins. "You're fucking Chase Adams. Your father—"

"Don't."

He stops, and I glance around, hoping Sawyer isn't within ear shot. "You don't want anyone to know?" he asks.

"Yeah, something like that. Can we keep this between us for now?" Jesus, Sawyer needs to hear it from me, not our new friends.

"Sawyer doesn't know, huh?"

"No."

He shakes his head, incredulous. "I thought you two were the real deal, a love at first sight kind of thing, but I guess I was wrong."

"You're not wrong. I really like her, Trev. I just...wanted her to get to know me. People act differently when they find out who I am, who my dad is."

He frowns and nods. "I can understand that. You're kind of a celebrity."

I give a half laugh half snort. "I don't want to be a celebrity. I just want to play hockey."

"I'm afraid that's not how it works."

"Don't I know it." I look around the room and catch Sawyer's eyes. She smiles at me and my heart thumps a bit harder as worry grips me by the balls. "Do you think she'll be upset that I didn't tell her?"

"I guess there's only one way to find out."

He's right, there is only one way. Which means, I need to tell her the truth, but when...and how? Do I do it now, and ruin what could be our last night together, or do I do it in the morning, and hope for the best?

18

SAWYER

The fire in the hearth starts to die down, and while it looks like this party to celebrate our last night together is in no hurry to wind down, I'm anxious to get back to our room and have some alone time with Chase. He's been occupied all night, chatting with Trevor and the others, as I'm bombarded with questions about my play. Every time I caught his eye, he seemed a bit anxious about something. Maybe he's just restless, ready to get out of here and to Halifax to get on with his vacation. He did ask me to show him around. Was that just chatter or does he really want that?

I excuse myself from the group and make my way to him. His smile, which is always confident and at the ready, falters a bit when I approach. Jeez, now that we're getting out of here, is he pulling back, giving me signals that when this is done, we're done? Unease mushrooms inside me and I try not to appear a bit shaken up by that last thought. I yawn and stretch my arms.

"I'm going to head up." He nods, and when he doesn't respond, I jerk my thumb toward the stairs. "I'll just go then." I guess he's not in a hurry, and maybe he doesn't even want to come up. Maybe our time is over tonight, instead of tomorrow.

He sets his beer bottle on the end table. "I'm coming."

My heart jumps a little, a warning that come morning, it could very well be split in two. But I don't want to think about that. I have tonight with Chase, and I want to enjoy that before trying to figure out what tomorrow brings.

He puts his hand on the small of my back, and shivers go through me as he flattens his palm and guides me through the crowd, toward the stairs. We both fall quiet, lost in our own thoughts as we ascend the stairs, the voices in the main lobby growing faint.

I work to quiet my racing heart as well as my racing brain as I steal a fast glance at Chase. His brow is furrowed, and his jaw is clenched in a way that says he's deep in thought, concerned about something. We reach our room, and his energy, anxiety, fills the space as I open the door.

"What's up?" I ask as we step inside, my own nerves a bit jumbled.

He stares at me for a second and I take a breath and hold it. I'm not sure what's going on with him—is he ending this?—but I'm bracing myself for the worst. He glances over my shoulders, and his gaze settles on the bed. A beat passes and then suddenly, his demeanor changes, lightens, and the playful Chase I've fallen for is back, standing over me, looking at me like he wants to devour me—one last time.

Chase sets the lock and I flick on the lights. "Nice to uh... have lights," I say for lack of anything else, and don't miss the way my voice is cracking.

He turns the lights off, but not before I catch the want in his eyes.

"We don't need lights," he says, his deep voice falling over my body and raising the hairs on my arms.

"No?" He slides an arm around my waist.

"I want to feel my way around."

Heat zaps through me. "I kind of like the sound of that." His big hands go under my shirt, his hot palms warming my flesh as he feels his way around my back, his hands going lower to cup my ass through my yoga pants. I'm glad I tossed them into my suitcase at the last second. Chase has been mesmerized by them all day, which I find rather amusing.

He squeezes my ass and groans, and I can't wait to see what position he wants to take me in tonight. How will he want to experiment and what will he want to teach me? He grips the hem of my shirt and peels it over my head. As light shines in from the moon and my eyes adjust to the dark room, I put my hands on his body, wanting to touch him, see him.

"While I like the idea of feeling my way around. I think I want to see you."

"I want to see you too, Sawyer," he admits, his voice low and rough and...rattled? What is going on with him? He flicks the light on and I wince, but my eyes adjust quickly and OMG, I haven't known Chase long, but I've never seen this kind of intensity in him before.

With his gaze zeroed in on my cleavage, he unhooks my bra and it falls to the floor as he frees my breasts. He cups them in his big hands and growls. "You are so beautiful, Sawyer."

"You are too," I say, and he grins, but the truth is, no man has ever made me feel beautiful and confident before, cherished even. I'm honestly scared to death about that. "And we can still feel our way around."

I tug on his shirt, and he inches back and peels it over his head. I've seen his body—felt his body on top of me, and beneath my fingertips—but this is the first time I've ever had a really good look and I like what I see. A lot. I run my fingers over the hills and valleys, enjoying the play of his muscles beneath my fingers. He growls and fidgets, as my fingers tickle rows of steel wrapped in feathery soft flesh. I move an inch closer and his scent curls around me, teasing the pleasure spreading through my core.

I tip my head up as he continues to massage my breasts, and there's a deep warmth in his eyes as he dips his head and kisses me. I expect hunger, a ferociousness in his kiss, based on the need backlighting his eyes, but the touch is gentle, soft, exploring, like it might be his very last taste of me.

Don't think about that, Sawyer.

I slide my hand lower, and cup his cock as it strains against his pants. Maybe this is all that was 'up' with him. Maybe old fears and insecurities are tugging at me tonight, assuming he's just going to up and leave, because I'm just not enough to keep him around.

He pushes against my hand and grunts. I break the kiss and ask, "Does it hurt, Chase?"

"Yes...fuck. I've been hurting for you all day."

Confidence bolstered, I grin, and release the button on his pants. He grips my hair and tugs, opening my mouth to his again, and I welcome him in as I release his zipper and take his big, hard cock into my hand.

His kiss, while still soft and gentle, has a hint of urgency to it this time, and I get the sense he's trying to restrain himself. If restraint is what it's going to take to make this night last longer, then I can get behind that.

I rub his cock, dip into his pre-cum and moan to let him know how much I like it.

"Baby, I need you naked." He drops to his knees and my hand slips from his pants. I moan in protest, but it turns to a moan of pleasure as he grips my yoga pants and peels them down my legs. I reach for his shoulders and hang on as I lift my feet one at a time so he can rid me of those pesky pants and underwear that are keeping his hands from my aching body.

He stays on his knees, and presses his face to my stomach. Inhaling deeply, he breathes me in as he cups my ass and holds me to him. My sex begins to flutter. My God, before him I wasn't sure whether I had orgasm or not, and now, here I am, ready to explode simply from the way he's holding me.

He presses hot, wet kisses to my skin, going lower to my hips and outer thighs. He taps my legs, and I spread them for him. He growls deeply as I offer him my pussy and he parts my folds with his fingers and softly swipes his tongue over my clit.

"God," I cry out, a little shaky on my legs. I reach out to grab the table beside me, and I grip the edge as his tongue centers on my swelling clit. Fire burns through me as he licks and I gasp as he slides a thick finger inside me. I glance down, and my heart becomes more engaged as I watch him lick and finger me. But it's the fact that he loves doing this to me that tugs at something deep inside.

My body begins to quake, little clenches around his finger, and he angles his head, his eyes on mine. "Feel good?" he asks.

"So good, Chase."

I let go of the table and grip his head, using it to hold his face to my pussy, to help me keep my balance. I grind against him, move my hips and ride his face as he fingers me. I lose my breath, catch it again, and begin to pant as pleasure builds between my legs.

"Chase," I cry out. "I'm...I'm..." My body lets go before I get the chance to tell him, but I suspect he was well aware I was about to come around his finger and spill into his hungry mouth. I lean forward, and he touches me lightly, drawing out the waves as I continue to clench around his finger.

A second later, just as I'm finally able to get my breath, he stands, scoops me up and his eyes are locked on mine as he carries me to the bed. I fall back, and shimmy to the center as he stands back, his pants still dangling around his hips, and takes his cock into his hand. He rubs himself slowly as he circles the bed, his gaze on my body, drinking me in from all angles. I watch, mesmerized as he stalks like a predator about to take down his prey. Or maybe he's trying to commit my body to memory because it's our last night together. My eyes drop to take in his raging erection. Okay, maybe he's doing math so this isn't over before it begins.

He shoves his pants to his ankles and kicks them off. "Spread, show me your pussy."

I gulp at his blatant, dirty command, and blink at him like I'm in shock, but I like it and he damn well knows it. "Show me your pussy, Sawyer," he commands in a soft voice.

I slowly spread my legs, my pussy missing his fingers and mouth, but knowing it will be filled with his gorgeous cock very soon. Once again, I'm kicking my ass for not spending my college years in bed—with this guy. I know that's ridiculous. He doesn't even live near me, but a girl can fantasize and really when sex is this good, I should have been enjoying it. Would it be as enjoyable with a different guy?

He goes to my bag, takes a condom from the box and sheathes himself and I whimper. "I wanted you in my mouth."

"Can't." The muscles along his jaw clench. God, I thought he was intense before but it's nothing compared to now. He looks like he's going to bust wide open.

I bend my knees, and crook my finger. "If I can't have you in my mouth, then I want you in here." I part my folds, and rub my finger over my pussy.

He growls loud and deep and his cock jumps in his hand. Moving to the foot of the bed, he climbs on, and settles on his knees. He moves closer, his big palms closing over my knees and pushing them open. I have never felt so exposed, so desired before.

"You need me to fuck you, Sawyer?" He rubs my pussy. "You need my cock in here?"

"I do," I pant, a desperate edge to my voice that matches his. He stays between my legs, just pumping his cock as he watches me. Is he going to take me like this, missionary style, or flip me over, put me in some crazy position and teach me something new?

He falls over me, bracing his weight on his arms beside me as his mouth finds mine, for a deep, tender kiss that finds its way into my heart. He inches back to see me, his gaze roaming over my face.

"Chase," I murmur, and snake my arms around his back to hold him to me. He cups my face, and moves his hips to position his cock at my entrance, and without ever losing hold of my gaze, he slides into me. I hold him tighter as he fills my body and my heart, and a low moan crawls out of my throat. He bends, kissing me to capture it, as our bodies join as one.

He moves his hips slowly, and his cock slides in and out of me, slowly and surely building pressure inside our bodies. His pubic bone rubs my clit with every thrust, and when I scrape my nails over his back, I'm sure I can feel him growing thicker inside me.

His lips find my neck, and he kisses me gently, a new kind of tenderness in the way he's taking my body. While I love the way he's taken me every time, there's just something a little more profound in this. Or maybe I'm feeling deeply because I simply can't keep my heart out of it anymore.

He pumps, and I rise up to meet him, and our bodies move perfectly together. He's in deep but I want him deeper, I want everything he's willing to give, and then some.

"Sawyer," he murmurs into my neck as a tremble wracks my body. "Jesus, that is so good."

I close my eyes to everything and everyone, except this man, and the way he's pleasuring every inch of me, body, heart and soul. In no time at all, I'm tumbling into another orgasm, and he's cursing under his breath as each clench massages his cock. His body begins to tremble, and he's hanging on, wanting to wring every inch of pleasure out of my body before giving in to his own. I love him for that.

I love him for a lot of reasons.

His head lifts, his intense gaze back on mine as my spasms subside. He picks up the pace again, and I hold him as each thrust is for him now. But he's not frantic or hurried. No, everything in what we're doing here is soft, warm, emotionally charged, and beautiful...

"Chase," I say as he grips my shoulders, and let's go high inside me.

"I know," he murmurs. "I know, Sawyer."

What does he know? That what's going on here no longer feels like two strangers getting naked to pass the time while stranded, or that we might have crossed the line here, going from a random hook-up to lovemaking?

19

CHASE

"**S**awyer," I murmur and lightly shake her. "Wake up. Someone's at the door and it sounds like the plow trucks are outside." As outside engines roar under the weight of the snow, Sawyer blinks, and my heart squeezes tight as a smile touches her face. "Plows are here," I say again.

She sits up and blinks, like she's trying to clear the fog from her brain as she glances around. Last night, I wanted desperately to talk to her, to tell her how I feel. I have no idea if I'll like the hockey or the academy in Halifax, and I'm not even sure I care. I want to be with her. I want to build on this snowed-in fling. I almost blurted it out, but was so goddamn worried she'd hate that I didn't really tell her who I was that I chickened out.

Dumbass.

The knock on the door comes again, and I jump up, tug on my pants, and hurry across the floor. I swing the door open to find Trev standing there. "Plows are here. We need to move our cars so they can clear the parking lot."

"Hi Trev," Sawyer says.

"Hey Sawyer. You might want to get on calling for a tow truck. It could take a while for it to get here."

She nods. "Good plan," she replies, but doesn't move. She can't. She's completely naked under the covers.

"Meet you downstairs in a minute."

I shut the door, and turn back to find Sawyer scurrying from the bed. She darts to the bathroom, and closes the door, and I have no idea why, but that somehow hits like a slap. With the contents of our bags everywhere, I begin to shove my things into mine, and she comes darting back out, flustered and panicked. What's her sudden hurry? Is she that anxious to get away from me?

"Hey," I say and put my hands on her shoulders. "Slow down." She opens her mouth but I press my lips to hers swallowing whatever it was she was going to say. "Can we talk for a second?"

She blinks up at me, and nods. "Listen I—"

Another knock comes, more urgent this time. "Fuck." I glance at the door and back at Sawyer. "Chase, you need to move your car," Harold yells.

Sawyer swallows. "You better go."

"Yeah, okay." I rake an anxious hand through my hair. "Can we talk later?"

She nods and my stomach tightens. What if, in all the commotion, I don't get to see her before we head back to the city. "I didn't even get your number."

"Shoot, we forgot to charge our phones."

I grin. "I guess we had other things on our mind." A little smile curls up her lips as another knock comes.

"Sawyer. Betsy called CAA for you."

"Coming," she says quickly. She darts to the old desk, pulls out the motel notepad and scribbles her digits on it. "Here."

I tuck her number into my back pocket, and hesitate for a second, wanting to blurt out how I feel, but there are sounds of feet running up and down the hall.

She walks to her suitcase and starts packing it. "We better move."

"Right."

I grab my bag, toss it over my shoulder, and head to the door. "Don't take off before we can talk, okay?"

"Okay," she says, looking completely distracted, and worried about something. I'm worried too. Worried that I might not ever see her again. But she gave me her number so that eases my tension a bit. "Maybe we can drive back to the city together." Her head lifts a smile on her face. "I guess we'll have to see what CAA says first."

She nods and I head downstairs. The plow trucks are out front, and everyone is rushing around, moving their vehicles.

Betsy stands by the door, tugging her shawl tight over her shoulders. "Betsy," I say, and she turns to me.

"Chase, you better get out there. They need you to move your vehicle."

"Yeah, I know," I begin, my stomach tight. "Is CAA here yet?"

"No, they're on their way. Should be here shortly. "That's my Malcolm." She points to the officer guiding the cars away from the parking lot and down the hill. Malcolm meets my eyes and gestures for me to come outside.

"I'll move my Jeep and come back inside. I want to check on Sawyer and see what's happening with her car and CAA and if she needs a ride to the city."

"She probably has to stay with her vehicle," she informs me. "That's the way it's done around these parts." She turns her attention to the parking lot. "You be careful out there, the lot is very slippery. Malcolm just about fell."

"Okay," I say and head outside. I trudge through the heavy, wet snow and reach my car. I brush the snow from the driver's side, climb in and start it. Once it's going, I drop my bag in the trunk and grab the snow brush. By the time I'm finished cleaning off my windows, I'm soaking wet, with the wind blowing the snow back in my face, and over my clothes.

The plow clears the snow out from behind my car, and because I'm rushing, wanting to get my car moved and back inside to talk to Sawyer before CAA gets here, I slip on an icy patch and land on my ass.

"Fuck me." I hurry to my feet, and jump into my vehicle, more blowing snow following me in. I'm cold and wet by the time I back my car from the spot, and catch Malcolm waving me to move along. I follow his command, waving my thanks, but as I get further and further from the motel, it's becoming painfully obvious that I can't turn back. The plows only cleared one lane so far, and there's nowhere on this mountain to turn around and go back. How far will I have to go before I can reverse direction, and how long will I have to wait until they clear the other side?

I continue for miles, and fish my phone from my back pocket to plug it in. I shake the water off it, and get it charging.

After what feels like an hour, I reach the bottom of the mountain and find another police officer directing traffic onto the highway.

I slow and roll my window down. "Is there any way for me to get back to the motel?"

"Nope, keep moving."

"I need to get back up there."

"Not today. It's going to take hours to get the people off the mountain, and get the roads cleared."

I'm about to argue, but he steps back, and waves his hand for me to take the ramp leading to the highway. "Motherfucker," I curse under my breath as I roll my window back up and follow his instructions. I pull onto the highway, drive out of his sight and pull over. I fish the scrap of paper with her number on it from my pocket and my heart sinks into my stomach when it comes out soggy, the numbers illegible.

I rest my head back, and my mind races. What do I do? I don't want her to think I just left without so much as a goodbye and I did ask her to wait for me. I also offered to drive her to the city. Christ, I hope she doesn't think I just fucked off, abandoning her on the mountain.

I sit in my car a little longer and watch the vehicles go by. Maybe I'll see the plow truck and can follow it. Time ticks by and I begin to consider that I might have missed them, or maybe the gas station was in the other direction. Just then my phone rings and my heart jumps as I answer it.

"Hello."

"Chase, what's going on?" Brandon asks.

"Oh, hey," I say, unable to hide the disappointment in my voice. I'm not sure why I thought it could be Sawyer calling. She gave me her number. I didn't give her mine.

"Nice to hear from you too," he snorts.

"No, it's not that." I exhale slowly. "I'll explain when I see you. I'm on my way now."

"Yeah, I hear they finally got power and you were getting plowed out."

"I'm on the Trans-Canada. I'll be there in a little over an hour."

"Drive safe."

I end the call, and watch the vehicles go by for a few more minutes. "Shit." I pound the steering wheel, and pull into traffic. All I can hope for now is that I run into her on campus, or someone knows her and can help me find her.

With Sawyer on my mind, I drive to the city, a little faster than I should and I pull up in front of Brandon's place a little after lunch. My stomach grumbles, a reminder that I haven't eaten today and I snatch my bag from the back and head to the front of the big dorm house shared by the hockey players.

The door swings open as I'm about to knock, and I grin as Brandon stretches out his arms and pulls me in for a hug. "Bro," he says. "Nice to see you in one piece. I called your folks to let them know you were on the way here."

"Thanks," I murmur. Shit, I never thought to do that. Sawyer is the one thing on my mind right now.

"Dude, you look like shit."

I shake my head and try to laugh off the worry inside me. "Why don't you tell me what you really think?"

"I just did. Didn't you get any sleep?" He looks over my face.

"Very little," I say.

"Sounds like it was a nightmare."

"Not entirely." He takes my bag from me and tosses it inside.

"You can tell me about it over lunch."

"Food, yes. I'm starving."

"First a quick introduction to Coach. He wanted me to bring you by his office as soon as you arrived."

He throws his arm around me and as we make our way down the steps of Storm House, I blurt out, "Do you know a girl by the name of Sawyer?" Honestly in a city this size I can't expect Brandon to know her.

His feet slow and he angles his head, his eyes moving over my face with deep concern. "What's her last name?"

I mentally kick myself for not asking. I purposely avoided it, for fear she'd ask me mine, and I didn't want her to put two and two together and figure out who I was. But fuck, the truth has to come out if we want to build on our relationship. "I don't know."

"The only Sawyer I know is Sawyer Jameson."

Hope fills me. "On campus here?"

"Yeah. She's Coach Jameson's daughter."

My steps slow. The coach's daughter? Surely to God, if Sawyer was the coach's daughter, she would have told me, right?

Did you tell her everything, dude?

Well, no, but why would she keep something like that from me. "That's probably not her."

"Not a very common name."

"No, you're right."

He holds his hand up. "Is she about this tall, dark hair?"

"That could describe a lot of girls," I say. "But yeah."

"Jesus Christ, Chase." He chews the inside of his cheek with his teeth as he looks off into the distance. His voice is low when he says, "What the fuck did you do?"

I swallow, hard, as my throat grows tight. "What?"

"She's off limits, dude."

"It can't be her." I shake my head, refusing to entertain the idea.

"Yeah, you're probably right." He claps my shoulder. "The more I think of it, the crazier it sounds."

"Why does it sound crazy?"

"She hates hockey players."

Fuck me sideways!

I stop dead in my tracks as the world closes in around me as air expels my lungs in a whoosh. What are the odds that there are two girls on this campus named Sawyer and they both hate hockey players? I'm not great at math, but by even my calculations the odds aren't great.

Brandon turns around and waits for me, and I ask, "Why... why does she hate hockey players?"

"I don't know. Maybe because her father is a coach or something. I think I once heard something about a bet, but I didn't pay too much attention to it. I just know none of the guys on the team will go near her with a ten-foot pole."

My stomach cramps, bile punching into my throat. Jesus, she can't be the coach's daughter, right? If she is, and the coach found out I was messing around with her, fuck...I can't even go there.

"Chase!"

I turn, and nearly get knocked over as Daisy comes running up to me. She jumps up and wraps her arms around me for a big hug. Like I said, we all go way back, and Daisy and Brandon are like family.

"Daisy," I say and give her a big hug. I haven't seen her since last summer, when our families were together at Wautauga Beach.

I set her down, and she looks me over. "Brandon filled me in on what happened. Glad you made it here safe and sound."

"Thanks, we're just headed to meet Coach. Can we catch up later, over drinks?"

"You bet, text me. I want to hear all the details about you getting stuck up on the mountain. I gotta run, but drinks at the campus pub later." She blows me a kiss as she takes off. Her long blonde curls bounce over her shoulders as she glances back and says, "Miss you, bro."

"Miss you too, Daisy."

"Bye, Brandon," she calls out before she disappears around the side of the house.

"Later, Daisy," he says and laughs. "Still the same old Daisy, always on the go and into everyone's business."

I nod and smile, longing circling my heart. "I've missed you guys."

"If you move here and join the team, you'll see us all the time."

I laugh, my thoughts going back to Sawyer. Maybe I should have asked Daisy if she knew her. I suppose I can do that later over drinks. I glance up and for the quickest of seconds, I think I see Sawyer, sitting in the passenger seat of an old Toyota. The car rounds the corner and disappears, and I shake my head, sure I'm seeing things. Wishful thinking, I guess. She's probably at some garage, arranging to get her car fixed—and wondering why I didn't go back to see her at the motel. Although, she probably figured out I couldn't go back, since they only cleared half the road. Still, she must be wondering why I haven't called yet. Fuck.

"Come on." Brandon puts his hand on my shoulder to set me into motion. "We'll grab a bite to eat after meeting Coach, and then I'll show you around campus before we meet Daisy."

"Okay," I say and work to inject enthusiasm into my voice as my stomach continues to clench. Sawyer can't be the coach's daughter; she just can't be. As I work to convince myself of that, I make a plan to ask my friends to help me find her when we meet for drinks. We cut across campus and enter the sports complex.

"It's not as busy as usual. Lots of students have already gone home for the break." My boots echo on the floor as he leads me down a hall and stops, knocking on an almost closed door.

"Hey Coach, it's me Brandon. Chase is here."

"Come in, come in," a deep voice responds, and Brandon pushes the door wide open, waving his hand for me to enter ahead of him. With an indiscernible expression on his face, Coach climbs from his chair, and walks around his desk to take a seat on the edge. I expect him to break into conversation about my father, everyone does, but I guess Brandon's father was also in the NHL, and maybe it's not such a big deal to him.

"Nice to meet you, Coach Jameson." I hold my hand out to shake and he accepts it. "I've heard a lot of good things about you."

"I've heard about you too."

"I'm sorry I'm late. I got caught in the snowstorm."

He shakes his head. "Why would the government build the Trans-Canada Highway on Folly Mountain? Worst place to be in a storm. I know a few people who got waylaid by the conditions and missed out on their vacations."

Is his daughter included in that list of people, and didn't she use those exact same words to describe the Trans-Canada? I try to keep my hands from shaking. I shove them into my pockets as he sizes me up for a second, and I get the oddest sense that he's troubled by something.

Jesus Christ. Was Brandon right? Is Sawyer the coach's daughter? If so, did she tell him about me—about what happened when the two of us were snowed-in—and that I apparently ditched her when I was done with her? No that can't be right. She didn't know my last name or that I was a hockey player. Why then is Coach folding his big barrel arms across his chest, the muscle in his jaw tightening when he says, "How about you and I have a little talk."

FML.

Was that...Chase?

I crane my neck to look behind me as we drive past the frat house where all the hockey players live, party and do God knows what else. I'm tired, so it's possible I'm simply seeing things that aren't there. I look straight ahead as my mind goes back to the last few days at Folly Mountain Motel. This morning, Chase asked me not to go anywhere before we could talk. I waited until CAA came, and Chase never came back. But I quickly realized traffic was only going one way, down the mountain. But what I don't understand is why he hadn't bothered to call or text.

"What's that?" Kara, my good friend from drama class asks, as she stops at a red light, her brow furrowed as she turns to me.

Did I say that out loud? "Oh, nothing." I give a dismissive wave of my hand. Honestly, I'm not sure what I saw. I only caught a glimpse of some guy wearing the same coat as Chase, talking to Brandon, one of Dad's players.

The light turns green and Kara steps on the gas to get us in motion. "You made a strange noise."

"I did?" I stretch my arms. "I think I'm just tired and hungry." I lean forward and glance into the side mirror, just in time to see Daisy running and jumping into the guy's arms. At least, I think her name is Daisy. I've seen her around. She's on the girls hockey team, and we don't run in the same circles, but I've seen her hanging with the guys from Dad's team numerous times. If that is Chase, and I'm not convinced it is, how do they know each other?

My stomach cramps. Maybe they don't. Maybe Dad's protégé Brandon is hooking Chase and Daisy up. That's when it suddenly hits me. Chase was talking about visiting his buddy, Brandon. Was his buddy Brandon Cannon from Dad's hockey team? Blood drains to my toes. Brandon is one of the team's biggest players, on and off the ice. His father was a former NHL player. If that was Chase, and he was meeting the well-known Brandon Cannon here on campus, why wouldn't he tell me that?

I pull my phone from my pocket—I'd charged it in the tow truck and played around on social media, even posting a few pictures from the bonfire—and I'm about to check Chase out on Instagram only to remember that I don't know his last name. I go to Brandon's profile and scan it. He doesn't post much, so I'm still in the dark.

Was that Chase?

My mind races, and I wish I'd gotten a better look. I resist the urge to ask Kara to turn the car around and do another drive by the frat house. As Kara pulls up in front of my place. I tuck my phone away, deciding to do a little investigation when I'm alone. A part of me is a little worried at what I might find, and I still can't stop wondering what Chase wanted to talk about back at the motel. He'd once asked if I'd show him around the city. That lead me to believe he wanted more. Was he going to ask if there could be more between us, or was he going to tell me who he really was? Then again, I'm still not convinced that was him standing with Brandon.

Or maybe I just don't want to believe it.

"Thanks so much for picking me up."

"Not a problem," Kara says as she takes a drink of the gigantic slushie she picked up at the service station. "Want to rehearse later?"

"How about tomorrow. I just want to get something to eat, and go to sleep for a week." Kara no doubt thinks I'm tired out from my ordeal, but really, I'm tired out because Chase and I were up half the night exploring each other's bodies. My sex clenches in memory, my entire body craving his touch again.

She nods in understanding. "Sounds good."

I climb from the car, get my bag from the back seat and wave her off. I head inside, and don't bother to call out to Dad. I texted him earlier, and he was in his office, in a meeting. He offered to pick me up when he was done, but I'd texted Kara and she readily agreed to get me at the auto body shop. She'd seen my posts on Instagram and wanted to know who the hottie was that I was hanging out with. I hedged when she asked, not really wanting to share the details of my hook up with the world.

Was it just a hook-up, though?

With unease coursing through my veins, I drop my bag, and head to the kitchen where I find some leftover lasagna. I scoff it down and go straight to my room afterward. I plunk down on my bed and glance around. Next semester I'll be moving out and rooming with friends. I've put it off because Dad would be in this big old house alone and I hated that. I didn't want him to think I was abandoning him, like my mother abandoned us. But it's time for me to move out, and we both know it. Maybe if Chase moves here, we could room together.

God, what am I saying?

I reach for my phone to surf through social media to see if I can find out more about Chase. The words blur as I try to focus, sleep pulling at me. I decide to close my eyes for a second, and the next thing I know my pinging phone wakes me. I blink, and glance out my window to discover night-time is upon us. How long have I been asleep? I snatch up my phone and see that Lily just messaged me. I read her text.

Lily: Omg, why didn't you tell me????

Me: Tell you what?

Lily: That you were snowed-in with Chase. I just saw your Insta photos.

My stomach tightens, and I sit up. How the hell does Lily know Chase? She's a huge hockey fan and if that really was Chase with Brandon...

Lily: Do you have any idea who Chase is?

Me: Just that he's from Boston and was coming here to visit a friend.

I try desperately to ignore the bad feeling mushrooming in my gut, but my efforts prove futile. I stiffen, and brace myself, because my intuition tells me I'm not going to like what Lily is about to divulge.

Lily: He's Jamie Adams's son. Jamie was an NHL player. Chase plays for Boston University, and is on his way to the NHL. He and Brandon go way back. I can't believe you didn't know this.

Me: I don't follow hockey.

My throat tightens, and my breathing grows a bit harsher as I try to wrap my brain around what Lily is telling me. Chase Adams is a hockey player, on his way to the NHL? My heart rebels, refusing to believe it. But my brain starts putting all the pieces together. I take a couple deep breaths, grasping for a different reality.

Me: Are you sure?

Lily: He didn't tell you?

Me: No, uh, it never came up.

I stare at the phone, as three dots appear. Why the hell wouldn't Chase tell me who he was, and if he plays hockey for Boston University why would he bring up moving here?

Lily: What did come up? (eggplant emoji)

Me: (Innocent face emoji)

No sense in lying. Lily knew my plans for Florida.

Lily: Oh my God, you slept with Chase Adams!

Me: Are you sure that's him?

Lily: Positive. I have no idea why he didn't tell you, though.

Yeah, me neither. I blink and glance out my window. What kind of game was he playing with me? I'm not sure I'll ever find out, considering he hasn't even bothered to text me. I didn't get his number. I didn't ask and he didn't offer. My heart races a bit faster. Maybe that really was him with Brandon, and he too is a player. Was I simply a girl to pass the time? The only available female around his age? An away game hook-up with a girl who's easily forgotten, because I'm not enough for him when there are more choices on the menu? Oh God, is this really happening? Is Chase that guy? I swallow the knot in my throat, not wanting to believe that. He was so sweet and kind and took such good care of me. I blink back tears, not wanting to talk about this as my emotions go on a roller coaster ride. Wanting to change the subject, I text back.

Me: How's Florida?

Lily: Awesome, wish you were here. Now stop trying to change the subject.

Just then, I hear the front door open and my dad calls out to me.

Me: I have to run. Dad just got home.

Lily: Fine, but I need to hear more about this hook-up. Message me as soon as you can.

I drop my phone and step into the hall, trying to appear normal, and not completely shaken up, my world crashing around me as I find Dad standing at the foot of the stairs.

"Hey kiddo, how are you?" he asks, giving me a big smile.

I lean against the wall, and smooth my hair back. I must look like a hot mess. "Good. Exhausted. Sad I missed Florida."

He frowns. "Sorry you missed your vacation. I know how much you were looking forward to it."

"Thanks." I was looking forward to the hot weather and hooking up with some random guy. I didn't get the hot weather, but I did get some random guy. Who, I *stupidly* caught feelings for. "I was just texting with Lily and she's having a great time." I try to make normal conversation, despite the fact that my heart is pounding hard in my chest. My dad angles his head and assesses me.

"Are you okay?"

I push off the wall. "Yeah, just tired, and in need of a hot shower."

"Why don't you go get a shower, and come down and chat. I want to hear all about your ordeal and your car."

I nod and head for a hot shower. My mind goes over everything that happened over the past few days, and about what Lily just told me. By the time I finish showering and dressing I'm a complete mess.

I take a breath and reach for my door handle when Dad's voice rises up the stairs. Is he talking to me? I'm about to call out to him when a murmured voice answers. Is he downstairs with someone? We so rarely have company and when we do, it's usually one of his recruits.

I pull open my door, and head downstairs, but the second I enter the kitchen, my world tilts on its axis. What the everloving hell? I stand there on shaky legs as my gaze locked with Chase's. He goes pale, the sight of me standing in the doorway throwing him off as much as the sight of him sitting at my kitchen table is messing with my every working brain cell.

"Hey Sawyer, I forgot to mention that we were having company for dinner. Sawyer, this is Chase. He's here to check out the academy and the team." My dad laughs. "Maybe you two already know each other, though. Chase was just telling me that he was holed up at Folly Mountain Motel too. What a coincidence, eh?"

"Ah, yeah," I say, unable to string a sentence together as I blink about a dozen times, hoping I'm hallucinating, hoping that Lily was wrong, but knowing I'm seeing clearly and my friend was bang on when she told me who Chase really was. "Coincidence." My heart is racing as fast as my brain, and honestly, it's a wonder I can even speak.

"Sawyer," Chase says, and swallows hard as his gaze goes from me, to my dad, back to me again.

"So, you two do know each other," Dad asks as he frowns, no doubt wondering why we're staring at each other like two deer caught in the headlights.

As I continue to gawk at Chase, my mind going over everything, it occurs to me that I don't know the guy sitting at my kitchen table at all. He didn't even tell me his last name. Sure, I didn't tell him my last name, or that dad was the hockey coach, but I just wanted him to see me differently. He was a hot guy who was interested and the last thing I wanted was for him to know that I was boring Sawyer, the coach's daughter—the same girl the guys on the team avoided at all costs. But to not tell me he was a well-known hockey player, that his father was in the NHL, and he was here to check out the team. That's just wrong.

As I stare at the guy I'd fallen for, old insecurities rise up and grip my throat. I guess it's true, and I really was nothing more than a snowed-in fling. That's when another thought hits and a tortured sound crawls out of my throat. I might not have known who he was, but maybe he knew who I was. Maybe

Brandon told him when Chase called him from the motel, and maybe someone on my dad's team—or at least someone thinking about joining his team—finally had enough balls to bag the coach's daughter and win the bet.

"Sawyer," Chase says again, his gaze still hopping between me and my dad. I get it, he's worried I'm going to tell my father what happened, and fuck up his chances of playing for the team. He might be an asshole, but I'm not.

"No," I answer. "We don't know each other."

21

CHASE

"Sawyer," I begin, again. I can't seem to get my words out past the big lump in my throat. She clearly thinks I ghosted her. Why else would she be saying she doesn't know me, hurt and betrayal filling her watery blue eyes. Wait, is she protecting me from her father? Worried that he'll kick me off the team. Is that it? I'm not sure but I don't even care about that right now. I just need to make things right between us. "I couldn't turn my car around and go back and I wanted to call. Your number, the paper. It got wet." I reach into my back pocket only to realize I left the paper in my car. "You have to believe me."

"What's going on here?" her dad asks. "Do you or do you not know each other?"

With her eyes still on me, disbelief all over her face, she says, "I thought I knew him, but I don't."

"Maybe I should give you two a minute," Coach Jameson says, and Sawyer moves to the side as he walks past her, leaving the two of us alone in the kitchen.

I jump to my feet and reach for her, but she pulls back. "You're a hockey player. Here to join the Scotia Storms." She flinches as the temperature in the room drops a few degrees. Shit. Shit. Shit. I wrack my brain, trying to fix this.

"I didn't tell you who I was because—"

"Because you had a bet to win."

I shake my head, panic erupting inside me as I try to figure out what she's saying to me. "Please let me explain."

"No, I get it." Her voice is cold and unattached, but the tremor in her hands lets me know she's just as shaken up as I am. "You had a bet to win."

"A bet?" I shake my head, completely confused. This isn't about me not going back to the motel, not texting her? "What the hell are you talking about?"

"What else did you lie to me about?" she snorts. "Are you really shy and introverted, Chase, or was that just an act, a way to draw me in?" An almost hysterical laugh catches in her throat. "Here you were pretending you didn't like the spotlight and couldn't act, but you win the Oscar for that performance. You fooled me into thinking you were a nice guy, but you're not. You're a hockey player who would go to any means, say anything to get me in his bed. Are you even into animal science, or did you think I'd like the idea of you being a sweet farm boy?"

"Everything I told you about myself was true..." Technically I didn't lie. I just didn't tell her I was a hockey player. I guess that's the same as lying. Fuck me.

"Drop it, Chase. I know all about the team's bet to bag the coach's boring daughter."

"Wait, what?" My gut twists. "You think I slept with you because you were a bet?" I yell, my voice rising in disbelief.

Jesus Christ, is that what she thinks of me? My throat squeezes tight as she stares at me, disdain all over her face. I back up, putting more distance between us, hardly able to believe what I'm hearing. Sure, I didn't tell her who I was because I wanted her to get to know the real me. In my gut, I obviously knew there was a chance she'd be upset, but to accuse me of something so vile...Jesus. Her accusations are hateful and hurtful, and maybe I'm the one who doesn't know her at all.

"Yeah, well, don't act like you didn't want it," I throw back at her. "Did you forget why you were going to Florida?"

Her hands ball at her side, and she glares at me. "I might not know who you are, Chase, but I do know you're an asshole."

"Yeah, well if you think I slept with you because of a bet, I guess I don't know who you are either."

"No, you probably don't," she shoots back, as her face tightens and hurt registers in her eyes. My heart stops beating as I see the damage my words just caused and I actually hate myself for hitting back, wanting to hurt her the way she just hurt me.

I reach for her. "Sawyer, wait. I'm sorry, I didn't mean—"

She flinches back, her face turning red, as tears fall down her cheeks. "Don't touch me."

"I think you should leave." The deep, angry voice comes from behind her, and I lift my head to find her father glowering at me. I open my mouth, desperate to apologize, and explain, but her father takes Sawyer by the shoulders and backs her up, clearing a path to the front door.

"Please—"

Coach Jameson points. "Go."

I storm outside, the cool winding hitting like a slap, but the sting from Sawyer's words have cut me on a whole other level. I walk to my Jeep, climb in and sit there for a moment, trying to get myself together. I should have told her straight up who I was. It was selfish of me not to, and now, not only will she not listen to me, she thinks I slept with her to win some fucking bet. Her father opens the front door, and I start my vehicle and drive off.

I drive around the city aimlessly for a bit, getting lost, but who cares. I was lost before I even got into the car. As the night grows darker, my phone pings and I pull over, hoping it's Sawyer, hoping she's realized I'm not the guy she thinks I am. I glance at the message from Brandon. He and Daisy are at the pub waiting for me, but dammit, I don't know if I can put on a smile and get through a pint.

Maybe I should just drive straight back to Boston and put this whole trip behind me. Obviously, that's what Sawyer wants, and I can damn well forget about joining the team here and registering for Animal Science. I fell in love with this place as soon as I arrived, and after talking to the professors in the science department, I knew this is where I wanted to be. Playing for the Scotia Storms was icing on the cake.

Goddammit, I really fucked this up.

I head back to the campus, park at the frat house, and walk to the pub. The place is loud and lively, a girl playing guitar and singing on the small stage.

"Chase!" Daisy shouts as I come in. She pushes from her stool and runs toward me. She's about to jump into my arms when she takes one look at me and goes still. "What the hell?" Her entire body stiffens as I work to keep from falling apart. "Are you okay?"

I scrub my face. "Not really," I manage to get out. I do my best not to drop and sob like a fucking baby.

She takes my hand, gestures to Brandon to follow and leads me to a quieter table on the other side of the room, away from the music. Brandon comes with three beers, sliding one to Daisy and me.

"Talk," Daisy orders, then exchanges a worried look with Brandon.

I take a long drink, trying to figure out where to begin. "I slept with Sawyer Jameson, Coach's daughter," I blurt out. I glance at Brandon. "You were right." Brandon frowns, unease on his face as I continue with, "It happened when we were both snowed in at the motel. I didn't know she was the coach's daughter and I didn't tell her who I was, because I just wanted..." I glance at my friends. "You know."

"Yeah, we know," they both say, and yeah, they do. They both have the same pressures as I do, considering their fathers were in the NHL with mine, and our families are all still close.

"I get it. I get why you did it, but Jesus," Brandon groans, gripping his beer glass. "This is all fucked up."

"Coach invited me to dinner to talk about my future, and he overheard Sawyer accusing me of sleeping with her to win some stupid bet I know nothing about, then he kicked me out. It's over." I lean back in my chair, everything I want now out of reach, but I'd give that up to have another chance with Sawyer. I fell for her. Hard.

"There is a bet," Daisy says quietly, putting her hand over mine and giving it a squeeze. "The guys all had bets on who could take her virginity. I heard about it from Jacob when we were seeing each other. I guess no one ever tried."

"Apparently, Sawyer knew about it," I say.

Daisy cringes. "God, that's horrible. I can't even imagine how that must have made her feel, especially when no guy would go through with it. What must she have thought?"

I take a deep breath, and as I let it out slowly, I consider everything I know about Sawyer and say, "It made her feel like she wasn't enough. That she's always overlooked. Fuck." I take another big drink, nearly finishing half the beer. "It's no fucking wonder she hates hockey players." I glance at my friends. "She wouldn't even hear me out."

"She was hurt," Daisy said. "That's probably why she reacted like she did. Under those circumstances, I probably would have done the same. Actually, I probably would have punched you in the face."

I stare into my drink. "That might have hurt less than being accused of bagging her for a bet. Her words not mine." I work to swallow down the lump in my throat, as I lift my head and glance at my friends. "I never meant to hurt her... I... love her," I admit. Christ, we had so much fun at the motel. Sawyer was honest and open and curious and genuine, so unlike any girl I've ever met. She never told me who her father was, but why would she? She had no idea I was coming here to check out the team. And maybe, after hearing about the bet, she wanted me to get to know her for who she was.

Brandon's voice breaks into my thoughts. "Maybe if you tried to talk to her again."

I shake my head, my stomach in knots as the image of her face, the wet tears on her cheeks flash before my eyes. "I can't go back to her house. No way will Coach Jameson let me near her."

"Maybe you could meet her somewhere else on campus," Brandon suggests.

"Yeah, I don't know." I push to my feet. "I need to get some air."

"Want us to come with you?" Daisy asks.

"No, I think I just need to figure some shit out. Maybe I'll just head back home to Boston. If I left now I could—"

"Hey!" Daisy captures my arm. "When did you become such a chicken shit?"

"What the fuck, Daisy?" I shake my head. Leave it to Daisy to tell me what she really thinks. Sawyer told me what she really thought about me tonight too. Daisy might be right, but Sawyer was dead wrong.

"Chase, out of all off us kids, you were the shyest and quietest, but that didn't stop you from always being the first to everything. You swung from the rope and landed in the water to show us all it was safe. You were always the first to stand up to the bullies, even when they were bigger and older, and you had the black eyes to prove it, but that never stopped you. You were always the first to lead by example and fight for what you want."

"Sometimes you were always the last too," Brandon pipes in and I turn my focus to him, not following along. "At the bonfires after telling scary stories and everyone ran back to their cottages, you stayed back and put out the fire by yourself. You might be the quiet one, but you've always been the brave one, Chase. Now is not the time to run the other way."

If I wasn't so gutted, I'd smile at the memory of Sawyer being afraid in our room, thinking it was haunted. "What the fuck am I supposed to do? She won't listen to me. She said she doesn't even know me."

"Then show her who you are," Brandon says. "Everyone likes that guy."

"How the hell do I do that when she won't talk to me and thinks I did something horrible?"

Brandon rolls one shoulder. "I don't know. You know her better than we do. We'll help however we can, but you're the one who has to figure out what it's going to take."

"Yeah," I agree, knowing he's right. "I gotta get out of here." I make a beeline for the door as my friends' words of wisdom bounce around inside my brain. It's true. I am a fighter, but this is the first time in my life, I have no idea how to fight for what I want.

I step into the cold night, and laughter follows me out of the pub. I pull my hood up, and walk aimlessly, until I find myself back at Storm house. For a moment, I consider getting back in my car, driving to Sawyer's and demanding she listen to me, but I know her well enough to know I'd be going about it all wrong. I snort. See, I do know her. That's another thing she was wrong about tonight. But I hurt her and can't blame her for lashing out. Christ, I hated seeing her hurt and have to make this right.

So how are you going to go about that, Chase?

I head inside the house and go to Brandon's room. I plunk down on his bed and pull out my phone. But there are no messages from Sawyer. A groan crawls out of my throat. Did I really think there would be? She doesn't have my number, but I'm sure she could get it from her father.

I toss my phone, and in need of a shower to help me think straight, I unzip my bag. My breath catches in my throat at what I see inside. I bend to take a better look. How did some of Sawyer's things get in my bag? I guess we were both is such a rush to get to the parking lot, we weren't paying attention to what we were packing.

I stand up straight, my mind clearing, as a new kind of determination grips me. Goddammit, I know exactly how I can prove to Sawyer that what's between us is real, that I'm who I say I am, and that I'd do anything to prove it to her and make things right. I snatch up my phone and call Brandon.

"Hey," he says when he answers. "You okay?"

"Is Daisy still with you?"

"Yeah."

"Good, get your asses over here. I need help putting a plan together."

22

SAWYER

I wake with a headache—probably from crying myself to sleep—and glance outside to see fresh snowflakes falling over the city. I have no idea when Chase is going back to Boston—he'll leave, of that I'm sure—but I hope the roads are good for him. Yeah, I might hate him for what he did, but I don't want anything bad to happen to him on the highway.

My phone pings and I roll over, and pull the blankets over my head. I don't want to talk to anyone for the next year. Wait, do I hear voices downstairs? I strain to hear my dad's voice and work to identify who the other male voice belongs to. Is Chase here? I sit up, and angle my head, but they're talking too low, and I can't tell if it's Chase or not. Surely to God after Dad sent Chase packing, he wouldn't have the balls to show up on my doorstep. Then again, he's the only guy on the team with balls big enough to win the bet.

I sit up a little straighter, my heart racing. Could it be him. My God, I don't want that. Why then is hope rising up inside me? I groan and fall back on my pillow. I still can't believe he kept who he was from me so he could win some stupid bet.

Did he keep it from you to win a bet, Sawyer?

That thought has me jackknifing up again. Why the hell are my internal thoughts turning against me? The front door opens and I sit in my bed and listen for Chase's voice, but air leaves my lungs when I realize I don't recognize the other male voice in the room. The door shuts, and I tiptoe to my window, and glance out. Just then Brandon glances up at me, our eyes meeting. I gasp and jump back to hide, but that's ridiculous. He just saw me.

What the hell is he doing here? Yes, as the captain of the team he has meetings with my dad, but something in my gut says the meeting was about me. If he's trying to talk Dad into letting Chase on the team, he's wasting his breath.

After Chase left yesterday, the truth about the bet came out and my dad was furious. He had plans to talk to the members of his team and get to the bottom of it, but I begged him not to. I'm embarrassed enough as it is.

Weren't you the one who asked Chase about sex?

"Shut up, inner voice!" I yell out loud. But that inner voice keeps taunting me. Okay, it's true that I was the one who initiated sex. I wanted it. Chase wasn't wrong about that. He didn't have to throw it in my face, however, but he was right. I was determined to get rid of my virginity. So, if he was just a willing partner and not 'bagging' me to win a bet, why didn't he tell me who he really was? I mean, I kept secrets about myself for my own personal reasons. Maybe he had personal reasons too. Not that I know what they are.

Because you wouldn't listen to him!

Blood drains to my toes. Oh God, did I ruin everything because I let old fears and insecurities creep back in. My phone pings and I practically dive onto my bed to get it, hoping it's Chase. We need to talk, but if he is innocent, he's never going to want to talk to me again, not after the things I accused him of. I shake my head trying to figure out what's real and what isn't.

I read the message from Kara, checking in with me to see what time I want to rehearse. I moan and flop on my bed. I did tell her I'd do it today but how can I possibly run lines when my life is in turmoil. I don't think I'm that great of an actress.

Knuckles rap on my door, and I turn my head as Dad enters. "Hey," he says.

"Morning."

"I think you mean afternoon."

"Fine, afternoon."

"You want some coffee?"

I push up and brush my hair from my face, hoping my eyes aren't as puffy as they feel. "Coffee, yes." I kick my legs over the edge of the bed. "What was Brandon doing here?"

He goes quiet for a second and my stomach clenches. I pray to God he doesn't bring up the bet. I just want to forget about the whole thing and if I accused Chase of something he didn't do, I don't know how I'll ever forgive myself. I don't know if I'll ever find the truth out either. Dad won't have him on the team now, and again, that could all be my fault.

"We had some things to discuss."

I want to ask if I was the thing they had to discuss, but I'm not sure I want to hear the answer.

"Come on. You really look like you need a cup of coffee."

I snatch up my phone and decide to message Kara after I'm caffeinated and thinking more clearly. Although it could take the entire pot for that to happen.

I make a quick trip to the bathroom, and when I make it down to the kitchen, Dad is holding a fresh cup of coffee out to me, and my mind instantly goes back to the service station, when Chase and I indulged in a cup of java. He was so good with that dog Killer, or rather Buster. Maybe he wasn't lying about wanting to go into animal science. He talked rather passionately about it.

Stupidly, I take a moment to envision us on a farm in a nearby community, where I can open up my own little theater. I take a fast drink of coffee, hoping it will help wash those lovely thoughts away. Like I said, even if having sex had nothing to do with the bet, he likely hates me now, and I ruined any chance of us being together. Is that why he lashed out at me, because I'd hurt him with my accusation?

God, Sawyer, what the hell is wrong with you?

My phone pings again. What the heck? Why is Kara so anxious to run lines?

Dad glances at my phone. "Are you going to answer that?"

"In a minute." I drop down into a chair. "Dad?"

He sits across from me and takes a sip of coffee. "What do you know about Chase Adams?"

He crosses one leg over the other and his head bobs. "Basically, I know his stats, and who his father was, and that he was thinking of transferring here for hockey and an education."

"Okay," I say. I have no idea what I expected him to say. Maybe that Chase was a saint or something, a really good guy, and I had it all wrong. "Do you...know if he's still thinking of transferring? Would you let him?"

He goes quiet for a long moment, and instead of answering he suggests, "Maybe you should talk to Brandon. He knows Chase a lot better than I do."

Not going to happen.

The doorbell rings and I stiffen. "Are you expecting someone?" I ask Dad.

"Nope." He averts his gaze, and I'm not sure why he's suddenly acting all strange as he walks out of the kitchen to get the front door.

"Hi Mr. Jameson. Is Sawyer up? I've been trying to get a hold of her."

"Sure, come on in."

I push to my feet, and round the corner to see Kara coming down the hall. "What's going on?" I ask.

"I thought we were running lines today." She checks her watch. "We need to go, like right now."

I rub my hand over my face. I hope she can't see the swelling. I don't want the whole world to know what happened yesterday. "I just got up. What's the hurry?"

She's practically vibrating in her snow boots. "I just want to get going."

"I'm not dressed."

"I'll wait." Okay, not only is my dad suddenly acting strange, now Kara is too. She waves her hand toward the stairs. "Go get dressed."

When did Kara get so bossy? "Fine." I dart up the steps, dress and tie my hair back without brushing it and forgo makeup. It's not like I'm trying to impress anyone. I open my suitcase and search for my script, but it's nowhere to be found. Shoot, did I leave it at the motel?

"Do you have the script?" I call out to Kara, not wanting to print out another. My inkjet cartridge is low.

"Yup, got it. Now let's go."

I tromp back downstairs with very little enthusiasm and put on my coat. Before I leave, Dad pulls me in for a hug. "Break a leg, kiddo."

"Uh, okay." Yeah, everyone's acting strange.

We step outside and I lift my face, letting the snowflakes fall over me, but now every time I see snow I'm going to think of Chase. Great, I'm going to have to move to the Sahara, but with climate change, and my luck, it will probably snow there.

Since the theater department is only a few blocks away from where I live, Kara leaves her car in my driveway, and we walk there. Inside the building we head to the theater, but I slow when I hear voices.

"Sounds like someone else is practicing." I jerk my thumb over my shoulder. "We should go. Come back later."

"Nope." She tucks her arm in mine and practically drags me into the theater, and my vision closes in on me when I glance at the stage and see who's standing there.

"What the hell?" I blink sure I'm hallucinating, but nope, that's Chase and Daisy on the stage. What are two hockey players doing in the theater, on stage no less? I falter backwards when Chase turns his head, his eyes locking on mine. My heart jumps into my throat, everything I feel for him washing over me. Oh God, I don't hate him.

I love him.

And that just makes this that much harder. He turns from me, and glances back at the paper in his hands. "What is he doing?" I notice Brandon, and a few other people sitting in the rows watching. Chase must hate this, judging by the color in his cheeks and the way his hands are shaking. He's quiet and introverted and hates being the center of attention. Why then is he standing up there with Daisy, doing God knows what?

Chase says something to Daisy, and my head jerks back. "That's my play."

"I know," Kara says and nudges me. I walk on rubbery legs and drop down into one of the seats as Kara disappears. She plays Stefanie in the play, the one who gets pregnant with Caleb's baby. The one Caleb doesn't really love, but felt trapped by.

Chase glances over the paper and lifts his head to look at Daisy, who is clearly playing my part—Emily. Chase begins, restarting the play in the exact same spot he and I started when we were at the motel.

"It's true. She's pregnant, and we're going to get married."

Daisy takes a step closer to him. "But do you— Uh, I can't get these lines straight." She drops her hands, turns her head to the audience and zeroes in on me. "Sawyer, can you do your part? I suck."

"What?" I stare, dumfounded, not at all understanding what's going on.

"Get up here," Kara demands, popping her head out from behind the curtain and waving me up. I push to my feet and take the stairs to the stage. Daisy puts her hands on my shoulders and positions me in front of Chase.

"Okay, that looks better," Daisy says and hands me the script.

I stare up at Chase, my heart beating a million miles an hour. "How did you get the script?"

"It somehow fell into my suitcase," he explains, his warmth reaching out to me and seeping under my skin to curl around my heart. My God, I love him so much it hurts to just look at him.

He starts again. "It's true. She claims to be pregnant, and she wants us to get married."

I stare for a quick second, then realize it's my turn to speak. "Do you love her, Caleb? You can't..." I swallow hard, and choke up a bit as I glance down—like the scene calls for. "You need to be with the one you love. Tell me she's the one you love."

He steps closer and puts his hand on my face, and I glance up at him, my heart and soul a hot mess of emotions. His gaze briefly falls to the script. His eyes lock on mine again as he begins, "Stefanie, she's the one..." He stops talking, as Kara, who is playing Stefanie, comes on the stage. The two of them are supposed to exchange lines next, but Chase turns to me. "Stefanie, she's the one who claims to be carrying my baby, but you're the one holding my heart."

I swallow, and look at the script. Did someone change the lines. "I think you made a mistake."

"You're right, I did make a mistake." I lift my head and find intense blue eyes staring at me. Everything about him takes my breath away. "When I met you, I should have told you straight up who I was, but I didn't." I take a breath but find it hard to breathe as Chase takes my hand in his. "I wanted you to get to know me. Chase, the quiet guy who loves animals and wants a farm someday. You said you hated hockey players, and I wanted you to see who I was beneath the jersey, Sawyer. I wanted you to see me."

"I...I see you," I tell him, my words as shaky as my body as I try to hold back the tears. "I wanted you to see me, too. That's why I never mentioned who my dad was, or told you why I really hated hockey players."

"I see you, and I know you, Sawyer. I've always seen you, and known you. You're not a girl who can or should ever be overlooked."

"I know you too," I say and sniff.

Emotions dance in his eyes as he steps even closer. "I never meant to hurt you. I'd do anything for you. I want you to know that."

"You didn't have to do all this," I whisper and glance at his friends in the seats.

"You wouldn't listen to me, and since I couldn't tell you how much I care, I thought I'd show you."

"Chase."

He puts his hand on my face. "I wanted to rewrite the ending to this love story, one that gave us a second chance."

My heart crashes against my ribs. I can't believe he did this. It means so much to me.

"I'm sorry, Chase," I say and shake my head.

He frowns, panic spreading across his handsome face. "Please, Sawyer, give me another chance."

I give a hard shake of my head. "No, you don't—"

"Christ," he moans and runs a shaky hand over his face as he curses some more.

I reach out, and take his hand. "What I'm trying to say is you don't understand. I'm trying to tell you I'm sorry I accused you of sleeping with me because of some bet. I knew better. At least, I should have. You did nothing to suggest you were that kind of guy and you've been nothing but sweet and kind the whole time we were snowed in. You took care of everyone." Warmth moves into my face. "Including me." A small smile touches his mouth, like he too is remembering the way he took such good care of me in so many ways. "I let my imagination get away with me. I thought the worst, and that's on me." I sniff as tears fill my eyes. "I made a mess of everything."

"Then let's rewrite that too."

I take a breath, not sure we can. "My dad..."

"Brandon talked to him this morning and straightened everything out. He knew I was going to be doing this."

I take a second to digest what he's telling me. "No wonder he was acting strange." I shake my head and seek Brandon out in the crowd. We smile at each other. Maybe he's not as bad as I thought he was. I turn back to Chase, my heart beating hard as I ask the next question. "Does that mean you're on the team and staying here in Halifax?"

"It does."

Happiness wells up inside me. I'm so glad that my old fears and insecurities didn't ruin Chase's dreams. Something buzzes in the back of my brain, and I reach for it.

"Wait, did you say rewrite this *love* story?"

"Yes, Sawyer. I love you. I think I fell in love with you when I found you standing on the side of the road looking like the abominable snowman."

"Abominable! Are you saying I was repulsive?"

"Oh, is that what that word means." He smiles and produces that cute little dimple that I love. "Then I meant to say adorable snowman."

"That's better," I say with a laugh, worry falling off my shoulders and loosening the knot inside me as he pulls me close. I take a deep breath and work to pull myself together. I don't want to ugly cry on the stage with everyone watching.

"What do you say we go somewhere private and start on rewriting our ending?"

"No."

His head rears back. "No. Sawyer, I thought——"

I press my fingers to his lips to stop him. "Let's start writing our beginning."

Just then the curtain falls, thanks to Kara, and those in the audience start clapping.

He dips his head and kisses me. "You'll always be the leading lady in our story, Sawyer."

I cock my head, and bite back a laugh, even though I love what he just said, I still need to tease him. "Really, Chase?"

"Too sappy?" he asks with a laugh.

"You should stick to hockey."

He arches a brow. "Do you still hate hockey players?"

"Yes." His eyes narrow in on me and I poke him in the chest. "But there just happens to be one I love."

A big smile full of love and happiness spreads across his face and reaches his eyes. "I love you too, now come on, let's get started on scripting that new beginning." He lifts me up and I wrap my legs around him. "I think it opens with the two of us naked."

"Yes," I agree. "It most definitely does!"

He's about to carry me off stage, but stops. "Wait, did you walk or drive here?"

I eye him, not sure what he's getting at but then a smirk crosses his face and I know him well enough to know what's going through is mind. "Are you thinking about my underwear?"

He laughs. "Sawyer, I'm always thinking about your underwear. You're not the only one with a fascination with them."

"I do not—" I shake my head and grin, my heart full of love and laughter. I can't wait to see what the future holds for us and I know that no matter what life throws at us, we'll always support each other and our passions.

Oh, wait...

I'm going to have to sit at the rink again!

EPILOGUE

Chase

I'm exhausted after our exhibition game, but hyped from the win as I glance up from the chair I'm sitting on and spot Sawyer, Danielle and Trev walk into the campus pub. I wave them over, my heart beating a little faster when Sawyer catches my eye, smiles and waves back. We've been together since we met on Folly Mountain, and we just moved in together last week after getting engaged. Now we start our new school year, while we plan our winter wedding. For some reason Sawyer wants a winter wedding, and I guess it's because we met in a snowstorm. I'm game, and I have to say every day, I wonder how I got so lucky.

My pulse jumps as she keeps her eyes on me and cuts through the crowd, and honest to God, I love her more with each passing day. It was corny when I said she was the leading lady in our story, yet it's also the truth. This year she's also the leading lady in her plays, and has been looking around for the perfect spot to build her playhouse. I'll be heading off to the NHL in a couple years, but Nova Scotia will be my home base, and Sawyer is keen on the idea of us living on a farm.

My parents have warmed up to the idea. How could they not? Once they saw how happy I was studying animal science, they came onboard. Although, a big part of my happiness is Sawyer, and my parents love her, just like I knew they would. I'm just glad her dad believed Brandon when he went to talk to him and explained the situation. Coach never liked the idea of any of the guys dating his daughter, and I don't blame him, but he quickly saw that Sawyer and I were the real thing.

"Hey," I say when she steps up to me. I stand, and pull her into my arms, planting a big, hungry kiss on her lips, and Danielle and Trev laugh.

"Get a room already," Trev says. I fist bump him before he sits, and give Danielle a kiss on the cheek. Ever since Folly Mountain, the four of us have grown close, and we often eat at the restaurant where Danielle is working.

"Great game tonight," Danielle says.

I gesture for the bartender to bring a couple more beers, and spot my buddy Matt Morgan moving through the crowd. At least he's trying to move through it. All the girls are blocking his path, and he's playing up to them of course. He's known around here as the golden boy, likely because everything comes so easy for him. But he's a good guy. A hard-working farm boy from Alberta. We instantly hit it off when I joined the team, and we also have a few classes together.

He finally makes his way to our table and snatches up a chair and sits. "Great game tonight," Trev tells him and he nods, and takes a swig of his beer.

"You going to Chev's party tonight?" he asks me.

"Nah, I'm looking for a quiet night in." Under the table, I put my hand on Sawyer's leg. She closes her hand over it, and my entire body reacts. It's tradition to grab a drink after a game, and while I'm expected here, I really can't wait to be alone with my girl.

"When did you turn into an old man?" Matt asks with a laugh, but beneath that laugh, I spot something else. Is it loneliness?

"Don't be jealous," I shoot back and he snorts a laugh, but it's forced. His gaze goes to the stage, to where a girl is singing and playing guitar. I've seen her in the pub numerous times. She comes, does her set, and quietly leaves. She's gorgeous, and I don't miss the way all the guys look at her. Not me, I only have eyes for Sawyer. But the girl on the stage turns down all offers of drinks and slips away once she's done her set.

"Forget it," I say, and Matt's gaze jerks back to mine.

"What?"

"I don't think you're her type."

Sawyer takes interest and leans in. "Wait, do you like Kennedy?"

"Who's Kennedy?" Matt asks. My buddy is usually loud, and funny and sometimes obnoxious, but tonight his mood is different. What is going on with him?

"The girl on the stage," Sawyer clarifies.

"You know her?" Matt asks.

"Yeah, not well, but we've been in some classes together. She's in the music program here."

Matt toys with his beer bottle, twirling it on the table, trying to look casual, but he's not pulling it off. He's interested, of that I have no doubt. Honestly, I've never seen Matt interested in anything more than a one-night stand, so now my interest is piqued too.

"What's her story?" he asks.

"I really don't know. She keeps to herself, mostly. I've talked to her, and she's nice, but she always seems to be in a hurry to get somewhere."

Kennedy finishes her song and looks like she's about to take a break.

"Maybe you should go talk to her," Trev suggests and Danielle nods in agreement.

"You think?" Matt says and I've never seen him nervous like this before.

"Sure, if you want to get shot down in public," I say, and Sawyer whacks me. "What?" I laugh. "She turns down every guy who's ever approached. I'm just looking out for my buddy."

He offers me that grin that has girls handing over their panties. "You don't think she'll go out with me?"

"No." With all the girls who chase after him, why is he zeroing in on the one he likely has no chance with. Is it the chase? Or something else?

He wags his brows playfully. "Want to bet?"

"I'll take that bet," I answer, and when Sawyer whacks me again, I sit up a bit straighter. "No, wait, I won't take that bet. Betting is bad. No bets, Matt."

Matt laughs and nods in agreement. Some of the senior guys on the team, the ones who had that bet going about Sawyer are gone now, having moved on after their academy years, and I'm glad to know Matt was never in on it. Neither was my buddy, Brandon. It's a good thing or I would have had to kick their asses.

A loud bang reverberates through the room and we all turn to the left to see some drunk guy jump onto the stage. He walks over to Kennedy and hands her a drink, but she waves her hand and declines.

"What, you think you're too good for me?" the guy slurs loudly and glances back at his buddies, who are all laughing.

"Fuck," I murmur and pull Sawyer closer to me. Kennedy is saying something but her voice is low, so we can't hear, but she looks terrified. The drunk douche reaches for her, and she flinches back, but can't shake his hold.

Matt jumps to his feet and his chair flies backward. "Get your fucking hand off her."

Douchebag turns to us. "Yeah, what are you going to do about it, asshole?"

I stand, and so does Trev. But Matt doesn't need our help. He's a defenseman on the team and can hold his own on and off the ice. But the douche on stage has friends, and I wouldn't put it pass them to all jump Matt in an unfair fight. Trev and I won't let that happen.

Matt cracks his knuckles. "I'd be happy to show you."

He stalks toward the stage, and I turn to Sawyer and Danielle. "Go to the ladies room. Stay in there until I come and get you. Shit's about to get real."

———

Thank you so much for reading Sawyer and Chase's story. I hope you enjoyed it. If you want to find out more about Kennedy and Matt, check out **WARM UP**, book 2 in my **Scotia Storms** series. Also, if you're interested in reading about Jamie and Fallon Adam's story (Chase's parents) and Cole Cannon and Nina Callaghan story (Brandon's parents) check out **The Risk Taker, and The Playmaker** in my **Players on Ice** series. There are 12 books in the series and they are stand-alone titles. If you want to find a sneak peek at Kennedy and Matt's story, read the excerpt below.

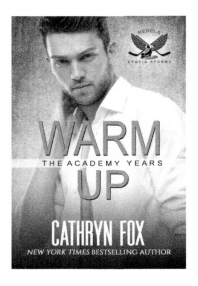

Warm Up

I briefly shut my eyes, blocking out the noise of the campus pub, and let the soothing sound of my guitar fall over me as I strum. Most of the time I'm up here on stage, singing and playing to myself, the students crowding the place too busy drinking, gossiping, or fighting to pay me much attention. Not that there is a lot of fighting. The owner Jimmy doesn't put up with that kind of nonsense, and once you're kicked out of the Tap Room, you're kicked out for the semester.

As I finish strumming, I take a breath and open my eyes, a rare sense of peace deep in my soul—that's quickly obliterated as I accidently make eye contact with some drunk guy at the bar. I normally don't play here after a hockey game. The place is always loud and rowdy, especially after a win like tonight, but there's no way I could turn down a gig. I need the money, and not just to play my tuition.

He holds his beer up to me in salute, and I set my guitar down, ready to take a break. I don't date, I don't have time for it. But I especially avoid drunk guys at the pub. Nothing good can come from that. I try to avert my gaze, and that's when it lands on Matt Morgan—not that I know him personally, I don't. But he's the star defense mam for Scotia Storms and his reputation precedes him.

His gaze goes from me to drunk guy, the back to me again as he inches forward in his chair, perched on the edge, like he's about to pounce. On the drunk guy, not me. But I don't want him involved. While I appreciate his gallant behavior—I really don't see much of that in the pubs where I play—I'm not worth him getting kicked off the team.

My heart jumps into my throat and I practically stumble off my chair as drunk guy jumps on stage, two beers in his hand. "Hey," he says, and hands a beer out to me. It sloshes over the side and I quickly move my guitar before he spills on it. "You look thirsty."

"I'm good, thank you though." I force a smile, and bend to tuck my guitar away. I'm supposed to play for another half an hour, but I want to get out of here before a fight breaks out, and judging by the way Matt and his friends all just jumped from their chairs, I'm about to be in the middle of a bar brawl, and not only do I not want to get hurt, or be the reason anyone gets hurt, I can't lose this job.

"What, you think you're too good for me?" the guy slurs loudly and glances back at his buddies, who are all laughing. He steps closer, sets one of the drinks on my stool and roughly grabs my arm. Heat crawls into my face, and I steal a fast glance around the bar as a hush comes over the crowd, everyone interested in the scene playing out on stage—with me in the middle of it. Kill me freaking now. I tug my hand away, or at least I try. His hand is the size of a baseball glove and he's got one hell of a strong grip.

"Get your fucking hand off her." My gaze flies to Matt. His murderous eyes lock on frat boy, and it's a good thing he's not directing that stare at me. I'd probably fall dead right before his eyes.

Frat boy smirks as he turns to Matt. With his attention diverted, his grip loosens and I'm able to snatch my hand back. I stand there, my heart crashing against my ribs. "Please stop," I say, but my voice gets drowned out by the guy standing over me.

"Yeah, what are you going to do about it, asshole?" he taunts, setting the other beer down, and fisting his hands.

"I don't want any trouble." I back up, and stumble on the microphone cord.

Matt cracks his knuckles. "I'd be happy to show you."

He stalks toward the stage, and I hold my hands out, palms toward him. "Please, I don't want any trouble."

Matt jumps onto the stage, and squares off against frat boy, but it's not a fair fight. Nope not a fair fight at all. While frat boy is big and tall, Matter is bigger and taller, and his body is pure muscle and strength.

"Back the fuck off and leave her alone," Matt says.

Frat boy snorts. "Or what?"

Matt turns to me, his gaze moving over my face. Something in his eyes soften as he takes in my fear. "Kennedy," he says and the fact that he knows my name momentarily shocks me. But that's not the only thing that has my pulse jumping. I don't think I've ever seen such kindness in a man's eyes before. "You need to get off this stage," he says to me, before turning to his buddies and gesturing for them to help me.

Boots hitting the stage reach my ears as Matt turns back to frat boy. "Listen I'm not going to fight you. You're drunk, and you'll only end up getting hurt. But if you bother her again, I won't go easy on you," Matt says and I'm grateful that he's not going to pummel the guy in front of me. I also like that he's not throwing around his brawn when he so easily could.

"Fuck you," frat boy says, and draws his fist back. Only problem is, I'm standing close, and his elbow gets me in the eye.

"Owe," I cry out, my hand flying to my stinging eye as I drop to my knees. With my eyes closed I can't see what's going on around me. I can only hear the commotion of Matt dragging the guy off the stage, Jimmy cursing as he comes running out from his office, and the crowd cheering Matt on as he drags a kicking and screaming frat boy outdoors.

"Pack it up," Jimmy says to me, as tears fill my eyes.

"It wasn't her fault," Matt's friend, and fellow hockey player, Chase says.

Jimmy waves his hand around. "You know the rules. You fight, you're out. None of you are welcomed back until the winter semester"

My heart falls into my shoes as my mind races. I can't lose this gig. I instantly begin to calculate my expenses. If I cut my food bill down anymore, I'll only be able to buy crackers. I swallow hard. I guess I've lived on crackers before, but there's more than me to think about these days.

"Jimmy," I say, plead. "Please. I'm sorry. It won't happen again."

"It wasn't even your fault," Matt says as he jumps back up on stage, and crouches down next to me. "Jimmy it wasn't her fault."

He folds his arms across his chest, a good sign that he's not open to hearing my side of things. "You know the rules."

My body shakes, despite my best efforts to keep myself together. Usually, I'm shivering because I'm always cold, but this time I can blame it on worry and fear. Matt's big arm goes around me, and he helps me to my feet. While it's instinct for me to pull away, for the first time in a long time, I lean into him, let his warmth push back the cold racing through my blood—which is so not like me. The last time I relied on a man, or trusted him, was a disaster. Why the heck am I doing it now? I can only blame it on the adrenaline dump and the fear cutting through me.

Jimmy points to the door. "Out now."

Matt's arm tightens, hugging me to him as he leads me to the three steps leading to the main floor. "My guitar," I manage to choke out, my throat so tight it hurts. I try to turn back. His hold tightens.

"My buddy will get it for you." I nod and keep my head down, completely mortified as I work to put one foot in front of the other and step into the dark night. The cool September air washes over my skin, and I take deep gulping breaths. Losing this gig might not seem like a big deal to Matt, he's the world's golden child who never had to work for a thing—at least that's what I heard about him—but to me, it's food on the table, and not just for me.

"I'm really sorry," Matt says, his gaze moving over my eye, which will likely be sporting a big bruise come morning. "I'll talk to Jimmy."

I nod, but we both know he's wasting his breath. He might forgive Matt, heck a star on the hockey team brings in business. No one pays attention to the singer in the corner. But if I'm anything, I'm tough and resilient, and prefer to take action over feeling so for myself, so that's just what I'll do. Tomorrow, I'll put on my big girl panties and find another job.

"Thank you for helping," I say, my little pep talk giving me a measure of strength.

"That guy won't be bothering you again."

"I...hate fighting." I'm a peacekeeper, and there's not much I can do about that. "I'm glad it didn't come to that."

As my eyes adjust to the dark, and light spills out of the bar as his friends come outside to meet us, I admire the color of Matt's eyes. I'm not sure I've ever seen such a translucent shade of blue before. It's no wonder he has a harem of girls following him around. He scrubs the scruff on his chin, and oddly enough, the scratching sound does the strangest things to my insides. I reach for my guitar, needing something to do with my hands before I reach out and see if that scruff is as rough as it sounds.

What would it feel like on my skin?

Whoa, where the hell did that thought come from? I quickly shut it down, and the truth is I'm well aware where it came from. Matt is one hell of a hottie, and the second I saw that genuine kindness in his eyes, it tugged at something deep inside me. The truth is, I'm lonely. Between my home life, school, and work, there's no time left for anything else. Not that I want anything else. I will absolutely not—I'm talking zero percent chance here—get involved with anyone. Especially an easy going, life of the party, responsible only to himself, guy like Matt. Bringing a guy like that into my life would only be disaster, and I have more than me to think about.

"Thanks," I say to his buddy Chase, and force a smile as I hug my guitar to my chest. "I...need to get going."

"Did you drive?" Matt asks.

"Yeah," I say but quickly remember I chose to walk tonight. It's nice enough out, and I want to save gas until I need it in the dead of winter. After losing this gig, I'm glad I made that decision. Plus, I like for my car to be at home, in case of an emergency.

Matt glances around like he's searching for my vehicle. "I'll walk you to your car."

I give a fast shake of my head, and simply say, "You don't need to do that."

The pub door opens again and out walks Sawyer, who was in my English class Freshman year, and her friend Daisy. There's another couple with them but I don't know who they are. Sawyer gives them a quick hug, and they say goodbye. Once they've rounded the corner Sawyer turns to me.

"Hey," Sawyer. "Are you okay?"

I nod. "I am." It's a lie. I'm not really okay. I haven't been okay for quite some time now, but that's my business and I'll get through this like I get through everything else. I'm a resilient East Coast girl.

Daisy jerks her thumb over her shoulder as her fiance and hockey play, Chase puts his arm around her, and Brandon— another hockey player—joins the circle. "We're headed to The Lower Deck to grab some nachos. Why don't you come with us?"

A longing wells up inside me. I want to go. I really do. I want to have a normal campus life, but that's not in the cards. "I can't...I just lost this job."

My gaze is on Sawyer, but I'm completely award of Matt at my side. I don't need to turn to know he's staring at me, his intense gaze assessing everything I say and do. I slowly turn, and my tight throat tightens even more as my eyes meet his. Wow, I'm pretty sure no guy has ever gazed at me like this before. Being the sole recipient of his focus is rather unnerv-ing...flattering.

"Nachos are on me," he says. "It's the least I can do to make up for that asshole harassing you."

"None of that was your fault."

"Well, he's a guy and I'm a guy and I want to make up for our kind."

"You're not responsible for all mankind, Matt," I say, a little chuckle bubbling up in my throat.

He angles his head. "How do you know my name?"

I arch a brow and stare at him like he might have taken one too many hits on the ice. "Really?"

"You follow the team?"

"No," I say honestly. I don't. I don't have time. "I just heard of you. Who hasn't," I say lightly, at least I'm trying to be light. God, the last thing I want is for him to think I'm another one of his groupies. But a guy like Matt, he's hard to miss on campus.

"Don't believe everything you hear," he says, and Chase slaps him on the back.

"Only half of what you hear is true," Chase says. "The other half. That's true too."

"Hey," Matt shoots back, and pretends to punch him in the gut. Chase laughs, puts Matt into a headlock and rubs his knuckles on his head. The knot in my chest loosens as everyone laughs, the air flowing into my lungs a little easier now as the two fake fight like brothers, and best friends. I watch, transfixed, my heart squeezing a bit as a part of me longs for this kind of friendship, comradery...normalcy. Don't get me wrong. I don't regret the choices or my life, but this... I miss this.

I steal a fast glance at my watch. "Okay," I blurt out. The two stop playing around, and Matt fixes his mussed hair.

"Okay, you'll come for Nachos?" he asks, like me tagging along somehow just made his day. I guess she's really interested in making up for his kind.

I nod. I guess I was supposed to be playing for another half hour, which means no one is expecting me until my shift was over. What could one little plate of nachos hurt?

"Sweet," matt says and takes my guitar from me. I'm about to snatch it back, until I realized he's being gallant again. This time around, however, I'm older. I've seen too much and have been through too much to fall for a man because he's charming.

I hope.

———

If you want to find out what kind of trouble Kennedy and Matt get into, check it out here!

ALSO BY CATHRYN FOX

Scotia Storms
Away Game (Rebels)
Warm Up (Rebels)
Crash Course (Rebels)
Home Advantage (Rebels)

End Zone
Fair Play
Enemy Down
Keeping Score
Trading Up
All In

Blue Bay Crew
Demolished
Leveled
Hammered

Single Dad
Single Dad Next Door
Single Dad on Tap
Single Dad Burning Up

Players on Ice
The Playmaker
The Stick Handler

The Body Checker

The Hard Hitter

The Risk Taker

The Wing Man

The Puck Charmer

The Troublemaker

The Rule Breaker

The Rookie

The Sweet Talker

The Heart Breaker

In the Line of Duty

His Obsession Next Door

His Strings to Pull

His Trouble in Talulah

His Taste of Temptation

His Moment to Steal

His Best Friend's Girl

His Reason to Stay

Confessions

Confessions of a Bad Boy Professor

Confessions of a Bad Boy Officer

Confessions of a Bad Boy Fighter

Confessions of a Bad Boy Doctor

Confessions of a Bad Boy Gamer

Confessions of a Bad Boy Millionaire

Confessions of a Bad Boy Santa

Confessions of a Bad Boy CEO

Hands On

Hands On

Body Contact

Full Exposure

Dossier

Private Reserve

House Rules

Under Pressure

Big Catch

Brazilian Fantasy

Improper Proposal

Boys of Beachville

Good at Being Bad

Igniting the Bad Boy

Bad Girl Therapy

Stone Cliff Series:

Crashing Down

Wasted Summer

Love Lessons

Wrapped Up

Eternal Pleasure Series

Instinctive

Impulsive

Indulgent

Sun Stroked Series

Seaside Seduction

Deep Desire

Private Pleasure

Captured and Claimed Series:

Yours to Take

Yours to Teach

Yours to Keep

Firefighter Heat Series

Fever

Siren

Flash Fire

Playing For Keeps Series

Slow Ride

Wild Ride

Sweet Ride

Breaking the Rules:

Hold Me Down Hard

Pin Me Up Proper

Tie Me Down Tight

Stand Alone Title:

Hands on with the CEO

Torn Between Two Brothers

Holiday Spirit

Unleashed

Knocking on Demon's Door

Web of Desire

ABOUT CATHRYN

New York Times and *USA today* Bestselling author, Cathryn is a wife, mom, sister, daughter, and friend. She loves dogs, sunny weather, anything chocolate (she never says no to a brownie) pizza and red wine. She has two teenagers who keep her busy with their never ending activities, and a husband who is convinced he can turn her into a mixed martial arts fan. Cathryn can never find balance in her life, is always trying to find time to go to the gym, can never keep up with emails, Facebook or Twitter and tries to write page-turning books that her readers will love.

Connect with Cathryn:
Newsletter https://app.mailerlite.com/webforms/landing/c1f8n1
Twitter: https://twitter.com/writercatfox
Facebook: https://www.facebook.com/AuthorCathrynFox?ref=hl
Blog: http://cathrynfox.com/blog/
Goodreads: https://www.goodreads.com/author/show/91799.Cathryn_Fox

Pinterest http://www.pinterest.com/catkalen/

Printed in Great Britain
by Amazon